The Center Bench All-Star
Brian D. Campbell

Printed in the United States of America
First Printing, 2021

ISBN 978-1-7329161-7-3 (Paperback)
ISBN 978-1-7329161-8-0 (Mobi eBook)

Red Cliff Press
PO Box 371
New Boston, NH 03070

For My Old Friend, Jason

I'm so sorry I wasn't there

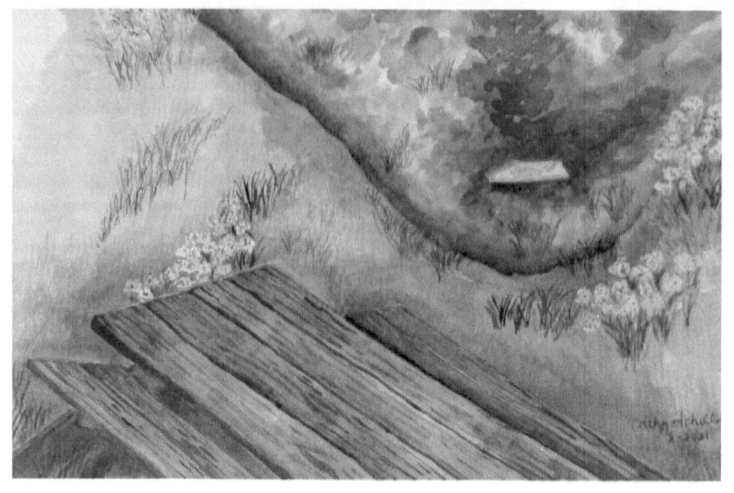

Chapter 1

I'd expected to be driving aimlessly across the country for a lot longer than ten hours. The plan was to meander along until I reached someplace no one would ever dream of finding me—or bother looking for me. I wanted to be as lost physically as I was emotionally.

In the days leading up to my wandering, I'd sold or given away all my possessions, bought a used pickup truck with a rebuilt engine, and set out—hopeful to escape my former life in Chicago.

I don't know if it was fatigue, I'd gotten off to a late start on my journey and it was half past midnight, or if something in my subconscious shouted that Lackton, Oklahoma was the perfect place to stop for anyone who wanted to be nowhere to be found.

Though I'd made up my beleaguered mind that Lackton was going to be my new home, and that decision was categorically reinforced while driving around looking for a place to stop and sleep, I had to make my way to the neighboring town of Kipford to find a suitable stopping point for the night—a Walmart parking lot.

I was too tired to drive and I was far too restless to sleep. That dreadful combination led me to spend the night sitting up behind the wheel of my pickup staring into the empty, dimly-lit parking lot remembering how perfect my life was before I'd started on this path to nowhere.

My life didn't start perfectly, though many looking on would have disagreed. I was an only child, living in Chicago, and my parents were wealthy. I was the product of an unplanned pregnancy and my much older than usual, first-time-parents didn't allow my unexpected birth to curb their gusto for living their best life.

Mom and dad were exceedingly generous with their funds, but dreadfully frugal with their time—and their love. My youth was overflowing with anything a child ever wanted, but brutally wanting of everything a child ever needed.

My parents' fun-loving and adventurous lifestyle led them to an inevitably early and tragic end. Ironically, it wasn't a hang gliding or skydiving accident that killed them, but a high-speed train derailment, in Germany, on my twelfth birthday.

After they died my only relative—an aunt on my mother's side—took me in. I don't know much more about any of the details of the crash and I've never bothered to investigate it further.

When people ask me about the accident I do my best to divert their attention by declaring it the deadliest train derailment in German history with hundreds of deaths. And then I add something like, "Germany has the most train derailments of any other European country. Best to take the bus in Germany, I guess."

I think it's true, but more importantly, that's typically enough to satisfy their curiosity, and happily change the subject away from my absent parents.

After my parents were killed, the next nine years of my life were quite different than the prior twelve. Aunt Evelyn, my mother's much elder and never-married sister—un-affectionately nicknamed Aunt Evil One by me and my new best friend, Charlotte —became my official guardian.

My new warden-guardian wasn't nearly as absent from my life as my parents had been. But I'd certainly wished she was.

Aunt Evelyn never missed an opportunity to proclaim to me, or anyone else who would listen, what a spoiled brat I was. And I suppose she wasn't wrong, but I resented her for saying it. She insisted that God had brought me into her care to turn me into a fine young man who would one day be a testament to her beloved and deceased younger sister.

With that, all of the luxuries my parents' money had bestowed upon me as a substitute for a lack of actual parenting were taken away. They were replaced with a pile of old books I was forced to read, a huge apartment I was forced to clean, and a frequent slap on the back of the head for any sign of ungratefulness I ever showed for my Aunt's willingness to raise me as her own.

All of this would have been far too much for a newly orphaned child to bear if it weren't for the previously mentioned, Charlotte. Charlotte, a girl my age, who I believed to be the most beautiful girl in the world, lived with her family in the apartment across the hall from my Aunt Evelyn's place.

Charlotte's upbringing was similar to my own until my parents had passed away, though her parents were a bit less absent. And though Aunt Evelyn wasn't ever shy about proclaiming that Charlotte was as much a spoiled brat as I was, she obviously admired the young girl almost as much as I did.

Charlotte was easy to admire. Aside from being the most beautiful girl in the world, she was perhaps the most polite and kind person I'd ever known. Aunt Evelyn was thrilled to allow Charlotte to come over as often as she liked to play with me and teach me a thing or two about manners.

My new best friend would help me with my long list of chores, and she would even read aloud to me when Aunt Evelyn had picked a book from the pile for me to start on.

During my first few years in Aunt Evelyn's care, I enjoyed nothing more than watching Charlotte read. And Charlotte actually loved to read—a passion I didn't pick up until much later.

Charlotte and I were inseparable through the remainder of our childhood and beyond. We both attended Northwestern University. I was a finance major and she studied environmental science. True to form, Charlotte wanted to save the world.

Six weeks before graduating, I'd already accepted a great job offer in the accounting department of a large sporting goods manufacturer in Chicago and I was feeling thrilled about the future.

Thrilled as I was, I knew there was still only one way imaginable to guarantee the perfect start to the perfect life. I proposed to Charlotte, and she said yes. My life was obviously going to be perfect.

Shortly after graduation, we mourned the passing of Aunt Evelyn, who I'd secretly become quite fond of. She was still crass and mean before she passed, and she never left me alone. But more importantly, she never allowed me to actually feel alone.

Aunt Evelyn taught me the importance of expectations. I learned it was much easier to succeed in life when someone you respected truly believed in you—and Aunt Evelyn truly believed in me. She also believed in Charlotte, but she wouldn't dare tell either of us any of that. It wasn't in her nature. Still, to me, it was as plain as a slap on the back of the head by a gentle old hand. It was obvious. Evelyn loved both of us.

Aunt Evelyn was my last surviving family member, but I didn't know how alone in the world I was at the time because of Charlotte. I was too busy settling my parents' and aunt's estates, and planning the perfect life, to give all of that any attention.

In time, Charlotte and I had turned Evelyn's large, empty Chicago apartment into a warm and pleasant home. I'd been promoted to Vice President of Finance at work, Charlotte had begun her dream job as an independent sustainability consultant, and our family was blessed with the arrival of our son, David, who had become the new spark that lit my entire world. There was no doubt in our minds. Our life was perfect.

I'm not sure if it's ignorance or arrogance, but so few of us ever realize how quickly an unexpected chain of tragic events can turn our perfect lives upside down.

Chapter 2

A startling crash on the rear bumper of my pickup had shaken me from a miserable, short rest in the cab of my pickup, which was still parked in the Kipford-Walmart parking lot.

It was hot—impossibly hot—for such an early hour, even in mid-June. I gathered my senses, wiped the sweat from my forehead, and slowly recalled where I was and why I was there.

A young employee who'd been retrieving shopping carts approached my window with a look of horror and shame.

My goodness, kid. I'm not going to bite your head off. What's the problem?

"Mister, I'm so sorry. The carts just got away from me. I'll let my supervisor know it was my fault. I think I put a scratch on your bumper. Mister, I'll pay for it."

I read the poor soul's nametag. "Ricky, slow down my friend. This old pickup has a lifetime of scratches and dings all over it. I really appreciate you taking responsibility for your mistake, good for you, but we don't need to get your boss involved."

Ricky finally exhaled in relief, but then he started up again, "But it was my fault. I'm really sorry."

"It's okay, I know you're sorry, but don't let this trouble you a second longer. Another scratch is just what this old heap needed for a little added character. Don't worry about it."

"Really? Are you sure?"

"Absolutely, but there might be something you can do to help me out."

Ricky just stared at me, confused, and tilted his head like a puppy who knew I was speaking to him but had no idea what I was saying.

"I'm new to the area. My name is Barrett Wentworth," I added, and offered the nervous young man a handshake. "I need to find someplace to rent in Lackton, the next town over. Do you know of any apartment complexes that might have some empty units? I just need to be pointed in the right direction."

"Well, sir, I live in Lackton, and I believe there's only one complex over there that ain't already full. But I'm pretty sure you don't wanna waste your time with that one, Mr. Wentworth."

"It's just Barrett—and I'm not picky or looking for anything upscale. If you give me directions, we can forget all about the new scratch on my bumper."

I followed Ricky's directions and made my way to the only apartment complex in Lackton with an available unit, stopping along the way at a gas station for the word's worst coffee and a pack of off-the-shelf, chocolate-covered donuts.

After parking my truck and taking a walk around what would soon become my home, I determined the scene at the Rolling Meadows Apartment Complex wasn't so bad.

There were ten buildings in the complex, and each of the two-story buildings consisted of twelve units— six at ground level and six on the top level. The buildings didn't have a common entry point with a shared hallway to each front door like apartments typically did back in Chicago. Every apartment had a separate entry point—the second-floor units had stairs to a front porch.

The buildings were old and run down, but they seemed to be occupied by families and good people— poor people, but good people.

There were children running around, enjoying the early weeks of summer vacation, shirtless and shoeless, with dirty little red faces.

I think this place will suit me just fine.

Every window of every occupied unit was open. Most windows were without any curtain or blind. Those that had blinds, had broken blinds, with one side clinging to the top of the window frame while the other side had given up years ago and remained unrepaired.

The buildings were dirty, but mostly intact. The grass between the buildings had bald spots all around—which were covered with loose dirt that released a cloud of dust into the air every time a shoeless child ran over them.

I could see that there were definitely empty units throughout the complex, so I decided to try and locate the leasing office to ask about renting one.

A woman with a deep southern accent called out from inside a nearby, open first-floor window, "Sir, are you looking for someone?"

I looked around, but the woman was too deep inside her apartment for me to see. "Yes, could you tell me where the leasing office is?"

"Leasing office? We ain't got no leasing office here. This is *Rolling Ghettos!*" the formless voice answered, and then followed with what I thought was far too much laughter for such a simple joke.

"I don't understand, ma'am. Is there someone I could talk to about renting an apartment?"

The invisible woman finally moved closer to the open window and came into my view. She had straight and greasy, dark hair with just a hint of silver, and was wearing a pink two-piece swimsuit that was about three sizes too small. It had possibly fit her well, in her prime, but she was many years past her prime.

She looked me up and down, and smiled. "It's miss, not ma'am. And you need to go and find Jasper. He lives in apartment thirteen, over yonder," she said, and then pointed to the building across the patchwork lawn.

"So, he's the manager then?" I asked.

Another hearty laugh, "Yeah, darlin', he's something like a manager—I guess. If he's not in his apartment, look under the hood of an old piece-of-junk Camaro out front. That car hasn't moved in years, or at least as long as I've lived here. That's 'cause ole Jasper is about as useful a mechanic as he is a manager."

I pointed to the building I thought she'd directed me to and asked, just to be sure, "That way?"

She looked me over again, slowly, and smiled. "That way, sugar. Bye now." She laughed a little more and then disappeared again inside the window.

"Thank you," I shouted, but there was no response.

As predicted by my future neighbor in the pink two-piece, Jasper was under the hood of an old Camaro—but it wasn't junk. It was a beautiful 1965 Camaro SS.

I waited for the barrage of salty words to end before announcing my presence.

"Excuse me. Are you Jasper?"

A man about the same age as me emerged from under the hood, covered in grease, and answered, "Yes sir, that's me. How can I help you?"

Jasper was a tall and fit man, tanned as a farmer, with bushy-blond, messy hair. He had a matching blond beard on his face, but he kept that meticulously well-trimmed and neat. The contrast was impossible to miss. He had kind, blue eyes and a laid-back, peaceful demeanor.

"You lookin' for someone, sir?" Jasper asked, after I didn't answer his first question. I was too busy admiring the Camaro.

I came back to attention. "Hi, Jasper, I'm Barrett. You know, a woman in the building over there told me

I'd find you working on a piece of junk? This is no piece of junk—not even close."

"I'd be willin' to bet you met Miss Tammy. Don't pay her no mind, she can be a little too bitter. Or sometimes a little too sweet—depends on her mood. She's just mad at me 'cause I won't take her for a ride. You be careful, Mr. Barrett, or she'll make a hard run at you too," Jasper added with a laugh. "Now, what can I do for you?"

"It's just Barrett. I'm looking for an apartment to rent."

Jasper froze for a moment. "For you? *You* wanna rent a place *here*?" he asked, pointing at me and then to the ground.

"Yeah, I'm new to the area. I slept in my truck last night, and I'd really like to have a bedroom to sleep in tonight."

Jasper squinted his eyes at me. "Are you lost?"

Though I'd had an answer for that question—a complicated answer—I just shook my head and replied with a smile, "No, not at all. I'm right where I need to be."

"Barrett, let me ask you a personal question. Are you in some kinda trouble? I mean, are you hiding from the law or something?"

"No, nothing like that. Of course not. I could submit to a background check if you want, or maybe give you some references. I have a clean record, I assure you."

"Well, all right. I ain't the FBI or nothin'. It's just you ain't the type that normally comes here looking for a place to rent, is all," Jasper declared as he looked me over. "We got good people in this complex—a lot of 'em are single mothers, and their kids. I gotta do what I can to look out for 'em."

Jasper and I chatted a while longer, and spent the next few hours together. Eventually, we came to an understanding, and I think he may have even become my first friend in Lackton.

He helped me pick one of the available apartments at Rolling Meadows, and then went with me to Kipford to buy a few furnishings to help make it more suitable for moving into.

My new landlord, and apparent friend, had attempted several times to ask questions about what the heck I was doing in Lackton, but he didn't press when I'd quickly changed the subject at each and every attempt. I could tell his mood about me had changed, slowly, as we spent the afternoon together. I think I'd won him over and he didn't believe I'd be any trouble.

The building owner, Jasper's boss, was a high school friend, and let Jasper live there rent free in exchange for collecting payments from the other tenants, kicking out the deadbeats, and doing whatever repairs he could handle—which unfortunately wasn't many.

Jasper owned his own pest control business, but business wasn't great. Living rent free was a blessing he couldn't afford to pass on.

After paying Jasper for six months' rent in advance, I asked him where I could possibly find a job—not because I needed one, I'd managed to build a large enough nest egg to live comfortably for a long time in Lackton. I figured I'd need something to keep myself busy. I told him I'd take just about anything—I didn't need a lot of money, I didn't want to be challenged, and I didn't want something that required much skill.

He said he knew exactly what I was looking for, and there was a good paying job available at a sawmill about ten miles north of Lackton. The foreman, a friend of his named Mike, was a little hard to handle for the weak or lazy, and he'd been having a hard time holding on to general labor.

Perfect!

Chapter 3

think it was my second, or maybe my third, weekend at Rolling Meadows when I first met Pippen Hammond. I didn't have much to do at the time, so I spent most of my weekends sitting at an old patio set that I'd bought at a yard sale and set out on the lawn. My intention had been for the set to be community property, but I'm certain I was the only one who ever used it.

It was difficult to gain trust at Rolling Meadows, espccially for the strange new guy who everyone had suspected was some type of outlaw hiding from the law. I'd sit out on the lawn under the umbrella, reading a book, or sometimes drinking a beer.

I was never much of reader until I moved to Lackton. Aunt Evelyn tried to force me to read as a child—so naturally I hated it. That is, of course, unless Charlotte was reading to me.

I'd never spent much time reading on my own until later in life. That's because after leaving Chicago, when

I wasn't reading or doing something else to occupy my mind, my thoughts would automatically return to the events that drove me away. So, I read all the time.

Jasper was the first person to join me at the patio set—most likely for a free beer—but it was a small price to pay for some much needed company.

"How's things going over at the sawmill?"

"It was a little tough at first, just like you said it may be, but I think I'm settling in. Mike doesn't yell at me nearly as much as he did when I first started."

"That's 'cause ole Mike thinks you're a genius," Jasper declared, looking at me with a grin. "He told me you was useless, like all his other help, till you figured it out and became his favorite employee."

"Well, I don't know about all that, but I'm doing better," I answered and then looked away.

"Yeah, you sure are. Anyway, Mike says you could run the whole operation if you wanted to, but he's sure happy to have you as a laborer. Says you're the only one he's got over there that he don't have to tell what to do all the time. Says you just know."

"I'm glad Mike's happy. I like my job—it would be great to keep it."

Jasper started to say something else about my job or my boss, but thankfully, for me, he was interrupted by an ear-piercing squeal from Tammy's open, first-floor window.

"Oh, Pip, sugar plum, aren't you the sweetest little thing in the world?" Tammy shrieked.

Her entire upper body was stretched out of her open window, and she was kissing and hugging a little boy standing outside, who looked like a baby gazelle caught up in the clutches of a hungry lioness.

Tammy released her prey after noticing me and Jasper staring.

"Hello, boys," Tammy offered in a seductive voice.

The same two-piece bathing suit she wore the first time we met was struggling to stay intact over her curvy body.

"I lost this here earring," she announced, while holding up a tiny silver half-hoop, "when I was sunbathing out there, near where that nasty table is now. I tried for hours, but I couldn't find it in the grass."

Jasper bit his bottom lip to hold back a laugh, and then whispered something only I could hear. "That pasty white skin ain't seen the sun in years. She was out here in the grass doin' somethin' all right, but it wasn't sunbathin'—I promise you that."

I gave my friend a horrified look, pointed at him, and raised my eyebrows.

"Me? Oh, dear Lord. No, not me!" he answered out loud.

"Anyway, this little angel of a darling must have heard me telling his momma how upset I was 'bout losing one of my favorite earrings, and he went looking for it."

"And I found it!" the young boy shouted with glee.

"And he found it!" Tammy repeated, and gave the poor little hero another kiss on the cheek.

"Pip!" Jasper shouted. "We'll save you from Miss Tammy, son. Come on over here, boy, and meet your new neighbor, Mr. Barrett."

"Bye, honey," Tammy said to Pip, while looking at me and retreating into her window.

Pip was a scrawny child—shoeless, like all the other children in our apartment complex—dressed in baggy shorts that he had to constantly pull up, and an oversized, white t-shirt with an image of some type of astronaut holding a pistol on the front. I had assumed he'd drawn that himself, with a marker, and wrote the title, *Space Lordz,* across the top. I don't think I'd ever seen him in another shirt.

He wore a cheap, worn-out baseball glove, constantly, and could be spotted nearly every day at Rolling Meadows tossing a ball straight up into the air, to himself, but rarely catching it on the way to the ground.

"Pip, Mr. Barrett just moved into our complex. Why don't you go ahead and introduce yourself, son," Jasper requested.

I'd expected the boy to stammer and stare at the ground while he did what Jasper asked of him, but he didn't. He walked up to me with the confidence of a grown man, looked me in the eyes, and reached out his hand for a firm handshake—as firm as could be expected from a miniature scarecrow.

"It's nice to meet you, Mr. Barrett. My name is Pippen Hammond, but everyone around here calls me Pip—except for my mother. You can call me Pip, too, if you want."

His words were as proper as his manners—no Oklahoma accent whatsoever. There was something peculiar about the boy. He seemed a little lost at times. I'd seen him all around the complex, but he never played with any of the other children. When he wasn't playing catch, with himself, he'd just sit in the grass, alone, staring into space for hours.

"Pip, it's great to meet you. I'm Barrett Wentworth, and you don't have to call me Mr. Barrett. You can just call me Barrett, if you want."

"Oh, his momma won't like that, Mr. Barrett. He's been raised to show respect to his elders," Jasper proclaimed. "Anyway, I'll let you two get acquainted. See you at practice, Pip," he added, and left us alone.

Pip was still standing in front of me, smiling, not saying anything.

"Practice?" I asked. "What kind of practice?"

Pip held up his gloved hand, "Baseball, of course."

"Mr. Jasper goes to your baseball practices?"

"Well, he *is* the coach. I sure hope he's there."

I smiled. I'd never pegged Jasper as the type to coach little league—never in a million years.

"Jasper doesn't have a kid on the team, does he?" I asked. I didn't recall Jasper ever mentioning he was a father.

"Nope. But we needed a coach and I guess he just did it. I think he's in love with my mother. So maybe he thinks I could be his kid one day."

I hadn't met Pip's mother yet, and Jasper had never mentioned any of that.

"You don't speak like you're from Oklahoma. Did you move here from somewhere else?" I asked, trying to change an awkward subject.

"Nope. I've lived in Oklahoma my whole life. Do you like baseball?"

I smiled at the alternate subject change and answered. "I love baseball. I'm a huge Cubs fan—just moved here from Chicago."

"If you love baseball, and you come from Chicago, you should be a White Sox fan," Pip declared.

"White Sox? Why's that?"

"Because only fair-weather, wannabe fans in Chicago like the Cubs. Real fans in Chicago root for the White Sox," Pip said with a smile.

I'd actually heard something like that on local sports radio while driving to work at the sawmill, but I didn't pay much attention to it. I'd been a Cubs fan since I was Pip's age.

"How old are you?" I asked, astonished by the young man's confidence and zeal.

"I'll be eleven next month."

My head jolted backward. He didn't look any older than eight. If he'd told me he was seven, I'd have believed him.

There was definitely something special about Pip, and I wanted to know him better. "You wanna play catch?" I asked.

"You don't have a glove."

"Good point. I suppose I'll have to go and get one. But until then, if you promise not to throw me any fastballs, I'll toss the ball with you," I offered.

"Well, I'm not a pitcher," Pip said, "So I don't throw fastballs. I'm an outfielder, mostly. That is, when Coach Jasper lets me play. If you throw the ball up high, I'll get under it and try to catch it. Then I'll just roll it back to you, so you don't hurt your gloveless hand. Would that be okay?"

After the thoughtful gesture from my fascinating new friend, we walked out into the grass together and spread out.

"You don't have to go too far. Just throw it up high," Pip requested.

I tossed the ball up as high as I could, and he tracked it down, got under it, but closed his eyes and moved away at the last second. The ball missed his glove completely.

"Maybe come a little closer, and not so high, at first. Let's try a few easy ones, so I can get warmed up."

I moved in a few feet, and tried again—same result.

I attempted to offer some advice about not being afraid of the ball, but Pip spoke before I could start.

"Mr. Barrett, I don't think you're a criminal. You don't seem like the type," Pip declared.

"Excuse me?"

"Everyone here thinks you're a criminal. They think you're in Lackton because you're hiding out from the police, or something. I think they're wrong."

I smiled at the kind-hearted little boy. "Thank you, Pip. I really appreciate you saying that."

Pip smiled back at me. "I think you're here to get away from something bad that happened to you. Just like me and my mom."

I didn't say anything. I was too flabbergasted to speak.

Pip continued, "I'm going to be your friend, if that's okay. I think I can help you get better."

I didn't know what to say. How did he know? Did Jasper tell him something about me? Then I thought about what else he'd said. Just like him and his mother? What had happened to them?

I was about to throw the ball into the air again, but noticed Pip had moved in to be closer to me.

"So what do you say, Mr. Barrett? Friends?" he asked. And then he put out his hand for another firm shake.

"We're definitely going to be friends," I answered.

Chapter 4

I stopped at a sporting goods store in Kipford on my way home from work. I wanted to buy a baseball glove so I could play catch with my new friend, Pip, and maybe offer him a few pointers. I'd planned on just getting one for myself, but then I remembered how small and tattered Pip's glove was— so I got one for him, too.

When I got home and thought a little more about the random gift, I decided it would be best to go and introduce myself to Pip's mother. I hadn't considered what she might think of a strange man giving her son a brand new baseball glove without occasion. I just needed to know which apartment they lived in.

I sat at my perch on the patio set, hoping to see someone outside who could guide me, but I was completely alone. I considered giving a gentle call into Tammy's window, or even knocking on her door, but I lacked the necessary courage to do so.

The easiest solution was to take a walk around to the front of his building and visit with Jasper, who was undoubtedly under the hood of his Camaro, cursing.

"Hey, Jasper, How's it going under there?" I asked, without looking to see if he was actually under the open hood.

Jasper didn't bother to look up. "Well, somethin' is goin', but that somethin' ain't this car. She still don't wanna start."

"I was hoping you could tell me which apartment Pip and his mother lived in—the little boy I was playing catch with yesterday."

There was an uncomfortable, long pause and then Jasper emerged, covered in grease, just like the first time I'd visited him while he was working on his prize possession.

He looked at me and tilted his head to the side. "What do you wanna know that for?"

"Oh, it's no big deal. I bought him a new baseball glove," I answered, holding up the evidence. "The one he was using was pretty much shot. I had told him I'd get myself one, so we could play catch sometime, and I ended up getting one for him as well."

"So, why do you need to know which apartment he lives in?" Jasper persisted.

I could feel an unusual tension in the air. Jasper was clearly uncomfortable with my questions. Maybe I shouldn't have bought the glove.

"I wanted to introduce myself to his mother before I gave him the glove—make sure she knew who I was, and that I was okay."

"Oh, man, okay. I'm sorry, buddy. I just couldn't figure out where you was goin' with that," an apparently relieved Jasper admitted.

I waited for him to tell me which way to go, but he just paused a minute, like he was thinking about something and needed to walk it through in his mind.

"You know what, why don't you just let me talk to his momma and I'll make sure she knows where the new glove came from. I'll let her know you mean well, and she don't gotta worry about you. I coach Pip, so we'll just talk it over, no big deal."

"Works for me. I just didn't want her to think I'm some creep."

"Right, that's a good idea," Jasper added while going back to work on the Camaro.

I started to walk away, but I couldn't help myself. "He's a funny little guy, isn't he?"

"Who's that?" Jasper asked from under the hood.

"Pip. I'd swear the kid was three years younger than he is, but then, when he talks, I'd swear he was ten years older. He's kind of an unusual little man."

Jasper came back out from under the hood. "He's autistic."

I didn't know what to say. There was obviously something different about Pip, but I'd never suspected a developmental disorder. "But he's so…"

"Smart?" Jasper finished my sentence.

"He's brilliant."

"High functionin' autistic. He's very special, and he and his momma are very special to me, too. You mighta noticed I was a little protective of them when you come over here askin' questions about where they lived."

"Yeah, I definitely picked up on that. I don't mean to pry, or get into anyone's personal business. I just wanted to play catch with the little guy."

"Of course, and that's fine. I think it's great that he took a shine to you the way he did. That boy don't ever talk to strangers like that, and he almost never talks to men at all. Shoot, he barely even talks to me."

"Really? I would have never guess that. He was so proper and confident when he introduced himself."

"Him and his momma, Sheila, had a hard time with his daddy. Pip's daddy is a real piece a trash—liked to get rough with both of 'em."

I just shook my head and pursed my lips.

What a jerk!

"A friend of mine and Sheila's took 'em in after the ex had gotten drunk one night and beat 'em both pretty bad. Eventually, the mutual friend and I helped them get a place here. Now I look in on 'em on occasion, and make sure they're okay."

"That would explain why Pip thinks you're in love with his mother," I offered, in a lame attempt to lighten the mood.

Jasper's mood didn't lighten. His expression remained unchanged—he just gave me a blank stare.

"Anyway," Jasper continued, "Miss Lauren, the mutual friend, comes around here pretty often. You'll probably like her. She's a little bit fancy, and stands out when she's here, kinda the same way you do. Between me and Miss Lauren, we take good care of Sheila and Pip," Jasper repeated.

I didn't know what else to say, and there was a long pause that felt like my cue to leave Jasper alone. "So, you'll tell Sheila about the glove then?" I asked.

"You betcha, bud," Jasper said, and then he disappeared under the hood of the Camaro.

Well, I think Pip was right, Jasper is in love with his mother, I thought to myself as I walked back to my table to wait for Pip to come around.

My friend didn't keep me waiting for long. He showed up moments after I'd sat at my table on the lawn—old, tattered glove in hand.

"Hi, Pip. How was your day?"

Pip ignored my question and got straight to business. "Hello, Mr. Barrett. Did you get a glove?"

"I did, and I have a surprise for you," I declared.

Pip's face lit up when I handed him the glove I'd bought for him.

"That's for me?"

"It sure is. It's going to need a little breaking in, but I'm sure we can work on that."

Pip put the glove on his hand, turned the palm side toward his face and began opening and closing it up. "I think it's gonna be just fine," he announced.

I tossed a few balls high into the air for him, like last time, and he dropped most of them, like last time.

"Can I offer you some advice?" I asked.

"You're gonna tell me to stop being afraid of the ball, aren't you?"

"Well, that and something else."

"Coach Jasper's always telling me not to be afraid of the ball. What's the something else you have in mind?"

"Well, I understand the fear. The ball can be scary. I mean, sometimes that thing comes at you pretty hard, right?"

"Yeah, they're not all lazy pop flies," Pip answered.

"That's true. But what do you think is your best protection against a baseball that's coming right at you?"

"This glove?"

"That's the perfect answer," I agreed. "That glove is going to keep you safe on the field—if you trust it."

"Trust a glove?"

"Yes, and trust yourself."

"Can you toss me a few normal throws? Nothing fast."

"I'd be happy to," I answered.

We played catch for almost an hour. Pip improved, and seemed to gain confidence with each throw.

"I probably gotta head home soon, for dinner. You wanna play catch again sometime?"

"Anytime, Pip. I'll be out here doing nothing all summer. If you want, we can work on ground balls next time. You wanna do that?"

Pip made one last catch, pulled off his new glove, and smiled at me. "See ya!" He shouted, and ran home, leaving his old tattered glove behind.

I think that was a yes to working on ground balls.

Chapter 5

'd never actually read any of J. R. R. Tolkien's books, but I absolutely loved the movies. And since I'd taken up reading as one of my dreadfully few pastimes in my new home—that and playing catch with my friend, Pip—I decided to take on *The Lord of the Rings* trilogy. I was sitting alone at my table on the lawn when a familiar voice called out.

"Don't you *ever* get tired of reading, sugar?"

I didn't look up from my book. I was hoping Tammy would take the hint, and disappear back into her window. She didn't, and I could feel her staring at me.

"Well, Tammy, it's a new hobby for me, and I'm starting to really enjoy it."

"I can think of lots of other ways to pass the time—ways that are far less lonely," she persisted.

I started to say something, but froze. My gaze lifted off the words on my book, but I didn't dare raise my head, or look toward Tammy.

Jasper warned me about this.

"Cat got your tongue, sweetheart?"

A welcome distraction arrived at exactly the right time. Pip was wearing his customary *Space Lordz* t-shirt and staring at my book.

"Hi, Mr. Barrett. What are you reading?"

"Hey, Pip," I answered in utter relief.

"Hey there, sweet Pip. How's your momma holdin' up?" Tammy asked.

She disappeared before Pip could answer—so he didn't.

I thought my words would confuse Pip, but I couldn't help myself, "Thank you, Pip. You have perfect timing. You really saved me there, buddy."

"She's not so bad. She's just lonely, and she doesn't have enough confidence to make new friends."

I looked at Pip, and smiled. *What an amazing kid.*

"I used to talk with her a lot, but my mom told me I shouldn't spend so much time around her."

"Your mother's pretty protective then? It's nice to have someone who cares about you looking over you."

"Yeah, she's a good mother. But I think she worries too much sometimes. What book is that?"

"It's part one of *The Lord of the Rings*. There's a character in here that shares your name."

"Pippin Took? Like most people, he spells it differently than me—with a second *i* instead of an *e*—and his real name is actually Peregrin. Most people don't know that."

I closed my book and shook my head with a chuckle.

"I'm actually not named after a hobbit though—in case that's what you thought. My mother named me after the main character from *Great Expectations.* That's her favorite book of all time. But do you want to know something funny?"

"Of course." *I really like this kid.*

"Pip, from *Great Expectations,* isn't really named Pip either. His real name is Philip Pirrip. He just couldn't say Philip Pirrip when he was young, so he called himself Pip. I guess it stuck."

"I guess it did," I agreed.

"You wanna play catch?"

"I thought you'd never ask. I have my glove right here."

"Do you want to come and see our field? We can play catch in the outfield if you want."

Pip pointed toward the woods across the street from our complex. "It's only right over there. There's a trail that takes you right to it. It's a short walk."

I hesitated. "Should we go tell your mom where we're going? I don't want her to worry."

"No. I go over there all the time. She'll know where to find me—if she needs me."

I followed Pip through a worn out and apparently heavy traveled trail in the woods between Rolling Meadows and a makeshift baseball field.

There was a pitching mound—technically. One side of the mound had been half washed away by rain, and the other was covered with weeds. There were old, half-rotten picnic tables on each side of the field, which served as dugouts, but they lacked any roof or cover for shade. The field did have a home plate, but no bases, or evidence of chalked foul lines around the infield.

"So this is where your team plays baseball?" I asked.

"Well it's no Busch Stadium, where the Cardinals play," Pip answered, "but it works for us."

"Is this just where your team plays?"

"Nope. Every team in our league in Lackton plays here."

"There's more than one?" I asked.

"Of course. We have twelve Little League teams in Lackton—six minors and six majors. We're an independent league though, so we're not very organized."

"Not an official Little League organization?"

"Nope. They have an official organization in Kipford. I mean, they have everything in Kipford, right? We just have Lackton Youth Baseball. But it's free."

"Well that's good. It's great that you kids get to play baseball in your own town."

Pip's eyes lit up, and he took a deep breath. "Actually, when our season is over, we put together an all-star team. The coach of the championship team gets to take two kids from each of the other five teams, and three from his own. Then that all-star team plays an exhibition game against the Kipford all-star team, before they go off to the state Little League tournament."

"Oh, that's cool. So the Lackton all-stars travel over to Kipford to play them?"

"No, no such luck," Pip laughed. "Kipford comes here, every year. And they slaughter us, and make comments about how crappy our field is, every year. Kipford's really good. They're good at everything over there."

We moved to the outfield and stated playing catch in the uncut grass and weeds.

"Pip you've gotten so much better," I proclaimed.

"Coach Jasper thinks so too. He let me play two innings last night. I'd never played more than one, before."

"Coach Jasper's a pretty good guy, huh?"

"Oh, yeah. He's nice. Sometimes I feel sorry for him though."

I stopped my windup and held onto the ball. "Why's that?" I asked.

"Well, you know how he's in love with my mom, right? Everyone knows that."

I laughed, and tossed the ball back to Pip. "Yeah, it's pretty obvious."

"Well, I don't think she feels the same. I mean, maybe she does, but I don't think she's ready. I hope she doesn't wait too long. Coach Jasper's a good match for her. Plus, I like him, a lot."

"You're an amazing kid, Pip."

We tossed the ball back and forth in silence for a while, before Pip asked a question.

"Did you ever play baseball?"

I sighed. "No, but I do love it. And I love my Cubs," I said. I remembered Pip's comments about how real fans in Chicago root for the White Sox.

I continued, "I'm more of a nerd than an athlete, unfortunately."

Pip laughed. "Yeah, I could tell. Someday you'll come around on the White Sox, too."

Before I could protest either of Pip's grave-but-true assaults, we were interrupted by yells coming from the infield.

"Hey, Center Bench! I thought we told you to stay off the field when coach wasn't here," a tall, lanky kid in blue jeans ripped at the knees shouted from home plate. He was flanked by three or four kids on either side.

"We need to leave," Pip announced.

"No way—we were here first. Who are these kids? Maybe we can play with them," I suggested.

Pip looked down at the ground, "That's my team," he answered softly.

"Your team is kicking you off the field?"

"They don't like me very much. It's not really their fault. They think I'm only on the team because of Coach Jasper, and they're probably right about that."

"Are you kidding me? You have every right to be on that team. And you have every right to be on this field," I protested.

"Can we go?"

"If that's what you want, then yes, we can go. But I still think we should stay."

As we were walking away, toward the trail in the woods, a kid from the group shouted to us, "See ya never, Center Bench!" The rest of the kids laughed.

Pip's demeanor hadn't changed, despite the insult and cruelty. He still had a smile on his face.

"They call me Center Bench because that's where I spend most of the games—on the bench. So I play center bench. Get it?"

"Have you ever tried to make friends with those kids? I mean, instead of just walking away like we're doing now? I think if you tried, those kids would see how great you are."

Pip's smile finally went away. "I'm not very good at making friends."

"Are you kidding me? You and I became friends in an instant," I declared.

"It's different with you," Pip said while looking away. "I can't explain it, but it is."

"Hey," I waited for Pip to turn toward me and continued, "we're gonna work on making some more friends, okay? Both of us."

Pip's smile returned. "I know. That's one of the reasons you and I have a perfect friendship."

When we made it to the end of the trail, on the Rolling Meadow's side, we were met by an angry woman, with her arms folded, glaring at both of us.

She was short, less than five feet tall, thin, and pretty. But at that moment it was hard to tell how pretty she was. She had a scowl on her face that could burn a hole into whomever she'd directed it toward. And she was directing it toward me!

"Just what in the hell do you think you're doing?" she asked.

I didn't know what to say. I just froze, and looked at Pip. Did he know this angry person?

"Mom, we were just playing catch at the baseball field. This is my friend, Mr. Barrett. He's the one who gave me the new glove."

"Pippen, I'm talking to him right now!" she shouted.

"Oh, goodness. You must be Sheila," I stammered. "It's nice to meet you. I meant to come and introduce myself, but Jasper…"

"Jasper! What about Jasper? You can't just give random gifts to children you don't know, and then go off into the woods with them. What's the matter with you? Pippen, get over here, now!"

It looks like Jasper never talked to Sheila about the glove…

"Goodbye, Mr. Barrett!"

Chapter 6

There was only one bar in the town of Lackton, and if you went there on a week night, or before the sun went down on a weekend night, it was safe—mostly. I actually found it to be a pleasant place to stop for a beer on occasion. And since I'd been mortified, by my own stupidity, with regard to my failure to introduce myself to Pip's mother before spending so much time with him, it seemed the perfect place to get away from Rolling Meadows—at least until things cooled off.

For most Lackton residents, Cattleman's Saloon, which was on the Kipford border, was the last stop on the way home after a night on the town in Kipford. Of the few brave souls who'd dared to venture through the door to check the place out, many never bothered to go back a second time.

I never stayed longer than it took to finish one pint of draft beer, but I did enjoy the charm of the place. It was like a step back in time to the Old West. The floor was worn out, unfinished wood and there was even a set of wooden shutters at the front door—like you'd see in a John Wayne movie. I could have easily traveled a little further, into Kipford, for more modern and comfortable surroundings, but Cattleman's suited me just fine.

I had just finished my customary pint, paid and tipped the bartender, and was about to push my stool back from the bar and head home when someone tapped me on the shoulder.

My heart was racing as I turned slowly to see who it was, but no one was there. Then a familiar voice said hello from behind the opposite shoulder.

"You're starting to feel right at home here in Lackton, aren't ya?" Jasper asked.

I took a deep breath and exhaled in relief.

"I know you'd never admitted to hidin' out from the law in Lackton, but now you're hidin' out at Cattleman's, of all places? And from teeny-tiny little Miss Sheila? Don't you go and deny it."

"Shouldn't it be called Cattlemen's?" I asked, in a desperate attempt to change the subject.

"Shouldn't you be sittin' at your table, back at Rolling Meadows, *all alone*, readin' a book, or somethin' like that? What the hell are you doin' here?"

"I feel like an idiot for not talking to Sheila before going to the ballpark with Pip. I know better than that."

"Come on, buddy. It's not that big a deal. Anyway, it's my fault. I was supposed to tell her about you, and the glove, and how Pip had taken a shine to you. I let you down. I'm sorry 'bout that."

"Thanks for saying that, but it's on me."

"Well, I talked to her yesterday and explained the whole situation. I told her you was a good man and that she ain't got nothin' to be concerned about. It's gonna be just fine—don't worry."

I shook my head and laughed. "I guess I'm making a little bit more of the situation than is necessary."

"Yes, you most definitely are. Now, quit beatin' yourself up, and buy us a beer, would ya?"

Chapter 7

I watched and laughed as Pip made his way toward me, at my familiar spot at the table on the lawn. He appeared to be on a secret mission, moving deliberately and quietly, stopping short of view from Tammy's window.

He waited a moment, to be sure he hadn't been spotted by anyone, and then waved his hand for me to come to him.

The little spy was carrying something unusual in his left hand, which for the first time in weeks wasn't covered with his baseball glove. He had a bouquet of local wildflowers that he'd picked and put together, and a notepad.

I'd gotten myself into enough trouble with my friend, Pip, but I played along and made my way over to see what he was up to.

Pip handed me the notepad and a pen. "I need your help. Can you write a note for me?" he whispered.

"If you want to impress someone with flowers, the note really should be from you." I whispered back.

"These aren't from me. Well, technically they are, but they're not. I need a note that looks like it was written by an adult."

"What are you up to, Pip?"

"These are for Miss Tammy."

"Miss Tammy is a little bit too old for you, isn't she? Heck, she's too old for *me*."

"I told you, they're not from me. And they're not from you, either."

"I'm willing to help you out, but you need to explain what you're up to."

Pip rolled his eyes and sighed. "I'm trying to help Miss Tammy, and I think I have the perfect way to do it."

"Okay, now give me the details."

"My mom teaches a free dance class once a week at the Community Center. My Aunt Lauren takes me there, all the time, and makes me dance with her so she doesn't have to dance with Mr. Mason, who's also there by himself, like Aunt Lauren."

"How does this have anything to do with Miss Tammy, or those flowers?"

"I'm getting there," Pip answered.

He paused and looked around. "And keep your voice down!" he insisted.

"Sorry," I whispered.

"Mr. Mason is a nice man. He can dance, too. He's really good—my mom talks about him all the time. She says all he needs is a dance partner, and he'd be the happiest man in Lackton."

I figured it out, "So you want to fix Tammy up with this Mason guy?"

"Yes! He's perfect for her. He's old, like her. He's a big, big guy—mom says he's a bricklayer— and Aunt Lauren hates dancing with him because he's got really rough hands. They both think he's the best dancer in the class though. Well, the best man dancer. He's super nice, and all alone—just like Miss Tammy."

"So, you want me to write a note to put with these flowers, and pretend they're from Mr. Mason?"

"Yes. That's exactly what I need you to do. Will you help me, or not?"

I wanted to tell Pip that it was dishonest, and could blow up in both our faces—and maybe cause his mother to never allow him to speak to me again. I still believe that was probably the right thing to do. But, that's not what happened.

I smiled at my partner in crime. "Let's do this!"

We discussed the note in great detail, and finally agreed to write something short, sweet, and to the point:

My Dearest, Tammy

Please admire these beautiful flowers as I've admired your beauty, from a distance, for some time now.

I'd heard Indian Blankets were your favorite, and I hope you like them. I'm sorry I didn't have the courage to give them to you in person, but I'd really like to meet you.

If you're ready for a little adventure, and willing to dance the night away, come to the Community Center on Thursday at 8:00 PM.

Wear your prettiest dress, don't mention the flowers or this note, and just walk right up to me and ask me to dance with you. The rest will be up to destiny.

I'll be the tallest man in the room, with all the best dance moves.

Will you be my beautiful partner?

Yours,

Mason

Pip's smile told me he approved of the note. "This is really good stuff!"

"Don't tell your mother I helped you with this."

"I won't tell anyone about it, at all. This is our secret. And it's going to work, too. I can't wait to see Miss Tammy dance with Mr. Mason at the Community Center. They're going to be so happy."

And with that, a very excited Pip went off to continue his mission.

I watched from my table as Pip snuck back around to the other side of the building, and made his way to the front door of Tammy's apartment, unseen by anyone but me.

He carefully arranged the flowers and note, laid them on the ground in front of the door, knocked loudly three times, and ran home as fast as his skinny little legs could carry him.

Chapter 8

During my time at Rolling Meadows, I'd only ever had one visitor knock at my door.

Early, on a Saturday, Pip and Sheila came over to invite me to breakfast. Sheila called it a peace offering for yelling at me about the glove and for spending time with Pip before introducing myself to her. To me, it felt like Sheila was looking for an opportunity to make sure I was okay before allowing her son to continue our unusual friendship together, and that seemed appropriate—so I accepted.

"Wonderful, we'll give you a chance to wake up a little bit, and see you in 'bout a half hour?"

"It's a date." I replied, and cringed—wrong choice of words.

Pip came running out of the door to their apartment to greet me before I made it close enough to knock.

"We made pancakes, scrambled eggs, bacon—and Aunt Lauren brought over about a million kinds of fresh fruits. It's like Thanksgiving in there!"

Aunt Lauren? I've been looking forward to meeting her.

"Sounds awesome, Pip. Let's get in there and thank your mother for such a great meal."

"And Aunt Lauren."

"Of course, and Aunt Lauren."

The layout of the apartment was identical to mine, but Sheila had managed to make hers much more appealing—with fresh paint and well-placed furnishings. They didn't have much in the way of expensive possessions, but they made a comfortable home with what they had.

"Welcome, Barrett. I don't believe you've met my friend, Lauren."

"I've yet to have the pleasure. It's nice to meet you, Lauren. And thanks again for the invite, Sheila."

Jasper was right about Lauren. She definitely stands out.

"Your spot is right there," Pip insisted.

I took a seat, as instructed by my young friend, and all three of my breakfast companions began bringing plates, and bowls, and trays of food to the table. Pip hadn't exaggerated. It was an impressive spread.

When the table was loaded to capacity, Pip sat to my right, and flashed a Christmas morning-sized smile. Lauren took the seat to my left.

Lauren and Sheila exchanged grins, and Lauren turned to me.

"So, Barrett, what brings you to Lackton? We know so little about you—you're quite the mystery man around here."

I'd prepared for plenty of questions, but Lauren was an unexpected twist. To say she stood out was an understatement. Lauren was stunning. She had a slender frame, long dark hair, and bright blue eyes.

I hadn't so much as looked at another woman since before leaving Chicago, and I'd not given the concept of attraction much consideration either. But, Lauren's beauty was impossible to ignore.

I drew a blank. I think I may have even developed a stutter. All of my rehearsed answers melted away, and I was left speechless and panicking in my own discomfort.

I sat there fidgeting with my fork, staring at the wall above Sheila's head.

"Aren't you gonna answer Aunt Lauren's question?" Pip asked.

I cleared my already clear throat and looked at Pip. I had no idea what to say, and I could feel all six of the eyes at the table piercing my skin.

This is NOT going to help clear any of the rumors about me.

Sheila turned her gaze from me and began to address her son. "Pippen, he doesn't have to answer, if he's not comfortable..."

"I'm retired!" I interrupted.

I'm what? Where the heck did that come from?

"You're retired?" Lauren asked. "You retired, and moved to Lackton? Where on Earth did you retire from?"

"Yes, I retired a few months ago. I'm from Chicago—lived there my whole life." It was mostly true.

"But Jasper told me you took a job up in Bilton—at the sawmill," Sheila replied.

"Yeah, that's true. I just wanted something to keep myself busy. It's a pretty easy job, and pay wasn't important."

Lauren shook her head and pressed on. "Okay, fine. But why Lackton? Nobody retires—at what, thirty?"

Thirty, huh?

I smiled. "Thirty-six."

Lauren smiled back at me and continued, "Nobody retires, at thirty-six, from one of the biggest cities in the country, and then moves out here—*to Lackton.*"

"Well, I'm somebody," I declared.

"You're *somebody* all right. But we're still trying to figure out who."

"Can I be honest?" I asked.

"Please!" Sheila and Lauren answered, simultaneously.

"When I left Chicago, I had no idea where I was going. I'd sold, or given away everything I owned, bought a used pickup truck, had it fixed up, and started driving."

"And you stopped here?" Lauren asked, in obvious disbelief.

"That's exactly right."

Everyone at the table stopped and looked at each other. They were checking to see if anyone believed my answer—no one did.

"I wanted to be somewhere that was nothing like Chicago," I continued. "And I found what I was looking for here, in Oklahoma."

"Well, that much is true. Lackton is nothing like Chicago," Sheila offered.

Lauren crossed her arms and looked at me with a smile. She wasn't satisfied, but she'd decided to end the interrogation—for the moment.

"You and I are gonna talk again, soon, Mr. Barrett," she warned.

"That would be nice," I replied, shocking myself. "But it's actually Mr. Wentworth. Only Pip can call me Mr. Barrett."

The mood at the table lightened, just a little, and we finished our breakfast.

"Mom, can I bring out my notebooks and show Mr. Barrett?" Pip asked.

"Yes, you may."

Pip took the napkin off his lap, laid it on the table, and got up.

"Stay here," he said to me, and then he stepped away and dashed down the hall.

Sheila stood and began clearing dishes. "Pippen writes his own stories. He's been asking me for days if he should show them to you, 'cause he always sees you reading out there on the lawn."

"Really? That's kinda cool, huh?" I asked Lauren, who was still staring at me with her arms crossed—her smile had disappeared.

"He's a kinda cool kid," she answered, blankly.

Pip came back to the table with a stack of notebooks, each with the title *Space Lordz* written on the cover, and each with a drawing that matched the one on his t-shirt.

"Just like your shirt," I declared.

"He does change his clothes," Sheila added. "He's got eight of those t-shirts."

"Wow, the drawing looks exactly the same on every single one of them."

"It's a decal, Mr. Barrett," Lauren added—arms still crossed.

"Decal?" I asked.

"I got a kit from Hobby Lobby," Pip explained.

"Of course. That makes perfect sense."

I would have sworn that was done with a marker.

"Remember when you told me you were more of a nerd than an athlete?" Pip asked.

Lauren and Sheila laughed.

"Um, well, you know. I'm not really sure I actually said that, exactly."

"You did. And that's okay. I'm kind of the same way. I love baseball, just like you, but I also like to write books. I've written five of them!"

"Five? That's amazing," I said and looked at Sheila. "This guy is amazing."

"Thanks. And since you love to read so much, I was thinking maybe you'd like to check out my books."

Pip handed me the stack of notebooks.

Lauren shot a glance at Sheila, who replied by shrugging her shoulders and nodding her head up and down.

"Are you serious, Pip? You want me to read these?"

"I do. I think you might be the only person I know who can give me an unbiased opinion about them."

An unbiased opinion? How old is this kid again?

"I can't wait to get started."

When breakfast was finished, I tried to help pick up the remaining dishes on the table, but Sheila insisted she'd take care of them. I thanked her for the wonderful meal, and thanked Pip for trusting me with his *Space Lordz* books—I promised to take excellent care of them and start reading as soon as possible.

Lauren walked me out while Pip and Sheila picked up, and I still felt like she didn't trust me nearly as much as the others in the room did.

"I really would like to talk to you again—alone, if you're up for it. They're like family to me, and I need to be sure they're okay."

I immediately lost focus, again, like I had at the start of our breakfast conversation. I didn't know what to say, and I started to walk away.

"Would you be up for that?" she persisted.

"Of course, I understand—anytime," I answered, and left Lauren standing there, with her arms crossed, watching me walk away.

Chapter 9

Despite the awkward moments at breakfast, and clear suspicion from his Aunt Lauren, Pip was still allowed to hang out with me and play catch.

He'd asked, multiple times, to go and play on the field, but I was still a bit tender after the last time Sheila met us at the end of the trail to the park. So, we played out on the lawn near my table and chairs.

I'd been waiting to talk with Pip about his books, so I started that conversation as we tossed the ball back and forth.

"I read your books."

"All of them?"

"All five of them."

"So, what do you think? Are they okay—for a kid?"

"Pip, I want you to know that I'm not going hold back or overpraise just because we're friends. You told me you wanted an unbiased opinion. Do you remember?"

"Yeah, I remember. Go ahead and let me have it then. I know they're not great, but I really like writing them."

"Your books are terrific. I mean it. You have a great deal of talent, and not just for a kid, either."

Pip just smiled and threw the ball.

"Have you been taking writing classes?"

He laughed at my question. "Me? Writing classes? I'm ten years old. I don't even know if they'd let me in."

"You don't write like a ten-year-old."

"You said you weren't gonna overpraise. I think you're being a little biased."

"Pip, I'm not. I'm being completely serious. I think you should show these to someone. I think, with a little work on your grammar, you could be a published writer."

Pip turned red and laughed again—louder. "Okay, Mr. Barrett. How about we just focus on baseball for right now."

"I'm telling you, you should..."

"Hello, boys," a familiar voice interrupted.

It was Tammy, but she wasn't speaking from inside a dark window. She was walking out of her apartment, toward the parking lot. Her hair was styled and clean, she wore a nice complimentary summer dress, and I think she may have been wearing makeup.

"Miss Tammy, you look amazing," Pip declared.

"Thank you, sweetheart."

"Miss Tammy, where are you off to?" I asked.

"Well, Mr. Barrett, I'm meeting a friend for an early dinner. We might even go dancing after. We'll see where the evening takes us."

Mr. Barrett? No sugar or sweetheart for me?

Pip looked at me and smiled. Had his plan actually worked?

"That's great, Tammy. Pip is right, you look lovely." She really did look lovely. She was the perfect after, for a before-and-after picture.

"Thank you, Barrett. That's nice of you to say. Y'all have a pleasant evening," she added before disappearing into the parking lot.

I looked at Pip and laughed. "Who was that pretty, polite lady?"

"That was the new and improved, Miss Tammy. We did that for her."

"You never cease to amaze me, buddy. If *that* is what our letter accomplished, we deserve a Pulitzer."

A new voice emerged from the direction Tammy had left.

"Did y'all see Miss Tammy?" Lauren asked. "She looked beautiful, and she was actually pleasant to me."

"Aunt Lauren!" Pip shouted, and he ran to her and gave her a welcoming hug.

"Miss Tammy has a date tonight," I announced.

Lauren's eyes widened and she leaned down toward Pip. "Ooh, I bet it's with Mr. Mason."

Was Lauren in on the plan?

"Do you remember, Pip?" Lauren asked. "She came to your momma's dance lessons last week, like she was on a mission, and then the two of them hit it off like they knew each other for years."

The letter actually worked.

Pip looked at me and smiled. "Yeah, I do remember that, Aunt Lauren," he said, and he paused, like he was thinking about it. "Huh, you might be right. It could be with Mr. Mason."

"Well, I'm gonna go say hi to your momma," she told Pip. "And then, if it's all right with you, I'd like to steal your baseball buddy for a chat."

Lauren turned to me, and added, "Would that be okay, Mr. Barrett?"

"Of course. I'll be right here, with Pip, until you're ready."

When Lauren was out of site, Pip declared, "She still doesn't trust you, but she'll come around—just give her a little time. She's more protective over me than my mother."

"Yeah, I'm not so sure about that. She seems pretty convinced that I'm some kind of shady character."

"Well, I think you two are made for each other, but neither of you has begun to figure that out yet."

I stiffened up and gave Pip a serious look. "Hey! Don't you go using your Jedi-level matchmaking skills on me. I'm doing just fine, young man. I mean it."

Pip laughed. "A *Star Wars* reference? Okay, boomer!"

"Boomer? I'm only in my thirties, and *Star Wars* is still cool," I insisted. "But hey, let me read your series a few more times and maybe then I'll be making *Space Lordz* references."

I pretended to be jovial with my friend, but inside I was a bundle of nerves. Another interrogation session with Lauren weighed heavily on my mind.

We tossed the ball a few more times and then when Lauren came back out to tell me she was ready for our chat, Pip said his goodbyes and ran home.

Here we go.

Chapter 10

L auren's tone and demeanor were noticeably softer than they were at breakfast a few days prior.

"Can we go somewhere? Maybe for a coffee or something?"

"I don't normally drink coffee in the afternoon," I answered. "I'll be up all night."

Lauren looked at me with a slight smile. It looked like she had tears in her eyes—like she had some horrible news to share with me and she was having a hard time getting to the point.

"I don't really want coffee either. I'd prefer a beer, actually," she admitted.

She drinks beer? With that figure?

"You're my kinda girl—how about we go out for a beer, and talk?" I said, and then I imagined myself trying to jump back over the line I'd just crossed.

"You have someplace in mind?"

"The only place I know of, around here, is Cattleman's."

"All right. That'll do. I'll drive."

We drove out to the edge of town, in awkward silence, and arrived at Cattleman's before dark—thankfully.

Lauren led us to a table, away from the bar, and away from any other patrons.

The bartender spotted us and shouted, "Lauren, sweetie, what are you and your friend havin', honey?"

"She knows you?" I asked.

"Most of them do, except maybe a few of the new ones."

"Come here often?"

"Well, it's been a few years, but I used to tend bar here when I was still at nursing school."

"You've gotta be kidding me!"

Lauren leaned back and smiled. "That was more than ten years ago. This place was a little bit nicer back then, but it hasn't really changed much."

"I don't even know what to say. I mean, I'd have never guessed you knew this place existed. I mean, Cattleman's?"

Lauren just smiled, and things became quiet. Eventually the sad look returned to her face.

What's on her mind?

"Shouldn't this place be called Cattlemen's, and not Cattleman's?" I asked, trying to get the conversation going again.

"How about Cattlewomen's?"

"I'd be fine with that," I declared. "I mean, that'd be better than Cattleperson's."

The bartender brought two draft beers over to the table and left us alone after giving Lauren a hug.

Lauren was the first to break the awkward silence left behind by the bartender.

"Barrett, I owe you an apology. A big one."

"You do? Have you done something terribly wrong that I don't know about?"

"I jumped to conclusions about you, before I knew anything about you."

"No, you didn't. You were protecting people you love. There's no harm in that. And by the way, to be fair, you still don't know anything about me."

"Well, that's not exactly true."

A shock went down my spine and I stiffened with fear.

What did she find out?

"I'm sorry, but I Googled you."

I looked at her in horror.

Why did I tell her my last name at breakfast?

"I'm so sorry. I had to know *something* about you. Your coming to Rolling Meadows was so strange. And your story about retiring out here just didn't make any sense. I found an article about your wife and son."

I looked down at the table, unable to look Lauren in the eyes. I considered running out of there, but she'd driven us and it was a long walk home.

Can I get an Uber out here in the sticks?

Lauren reached across the table and touched my hand. "I'll take you home now."

Sometimes the right gesture, from the right person, is all it takes to open your heart and allow you to let go, even if it's for just a moment. A little bit of tenderness can help to shake loose something that's been hurting you for a long period of time—even something unimaginable that you've bottled up for a year.

I desperately wanted to go home, but I didn't have a home to go to. My only home, in Chicago, was taken from me, savagely, about a year before that night.

I'd thought I could hide away from those memories, and the pain, and my in-laws who meant well but just couldn't let me forget about Charlotte and David.

My poor, beautiful, David.

I realized at that moment, with a practical stranger stroking my hand, that I had to release some of the pain that had been crippling me. I couldn't stand the idea of going back to my new place in Lackton, alone, and pretending the pain didn't exist.

"Can we talk a little more, first?" I asked softly.

Lauren bit her lower lip, and answered quietly, "Of course."

I swallowed hard and fought back the tears in my eyes. "We lived in a secure building, in Edison Park. That's the north side of Chicago, and supposedly the safest area in the city. We'd gotten pretty comfortable, and never bolted the door."

I stopped and noticed Lauren was still touching my hand.

"We had a lot of expensive things, and I guess we were an easy target for someone who was desperate, but we never gave that enough thought. We'd grown up spoiled, and believed no one could ever hurt us. Plus, we loved the city—Charlotte and I had both lived in that neighborhood our whole lives. We wanted our son, David, who was eleven at the time, to grow up there, too, and love it as much as we did."

Just saying his name forced me to release a few tears, but I felt like I had to continue.

"I'm sorry," I said, and then I took a moment to gather myself and clear the tears from my cheeks.

"Don't be sorry. I'm here. I'm listening."

"A young girl had gotten past the security door, somehow, and hid in the building until the middle of the night. She'd waited until it was late enough, and then she let a few guys in. She knew exactly where to go—she had pretended to be a steam cleaner salesperson a week before, and Charlotte had let her in to do a demonstration on one of our rugs."

Lauren pulled her hand back, and covered her mouth.

"I think Charlotte even bought a machine from her—that was Charlotte. She wanted to help everyone."

Lauren pulled her hand away from her mouth, placed it back over mine, and offered a half smile, though she had tears forming in her eyes.

"They'd managed to get into our apartment pretty easily. Like I said, we never used the deadbolt on the door.

"Two of the guys came into the master bedroom, and when I woke up one of them hit me in the head with a metal pipe. That's the only thing I remember about that night."

I stopped for a moment, and pushed my warm draft beer forward. I didn't want to drink anymore.

"When I finally came to it was late morning and the apartment was a mess. Anything of any value had been taken.

"My head was throbbing and bleeding, my ears were ringing, loudly. I stumbled around the apartment in a haze—barely able to stay on my feet.

"It took me a few moments to realize what had happened, and then I began to panic. Where were Charlotte and David? I didn't know if they were okay. The home invaders had left me for dead, but what about my family? Did they take them away?"

"Barrett, you don't have to…"

"I want to finish," I interrupted, with fresh tears on my cheeks.

I took a deep breath and continued. "I found them in David's room. They both had their hands tied behind their backs—and they were gone. Both of them were gone…"

I couldn't hold back the flood of tears any longer, nor continue. What more was there to say?

"Can you please take me home?"

Chapter 11

I kept to myself for a few days after sharing my story with Lauren—only leaving my apartment to go to work. At first I'd regretted coming clean, but she already knew my story. Silence wouldn't have made much difference.

After I'd had time to think about the night at the bar with Lauren, I began to realize how much better I felt. I hadn't spoken Charlotte or David's name out loud for over a year, and I'd avoided even thinking about the horror I'd left behind in Chicago since I arrived in Lackton.

It had finally dawned on me that having that release, and someone to talk to, was of great benefit to my mental health. I'd even begun to realize that I should reach out to my in-laws, to ease their mind, and let them know I was okay. But, I didn't go that far—at least not far right away.

It didn't take long for Jasper to come find me at my table when I finally ventured outside during my off hours.

"It's good to see you out of the house, Barrett."

I looked at the ground. I couldn't look Jasper in the eyes. "You know my story now, too?" I asked.

"It's a small town. I'd betcha everybody knows by now."

"How many people did Lauren tell?"

"Miss Lauren didn't tell me nothin'—at least not at first. My sister was tending bar the night you and Miss Lauren had your talk. She's the one that told me about your breakdown. Then I went to Miss Sheila's when I'd seen Miss Lauren was there. Miss Sheila and me got Miss Lauren to tell us the rest."

"Your sister? Jeez, this really is a small town."

"Yes it is, Mr. Barrett. But you don't need to let that scare you away to someplace else to hide from your sorrows."

I picked my head up, and looked Jasper in the eyes.

He had a sad expression, and a deep stare. Jasper was empathizing with me. "Matter of fact, I mean, the thing I came over here to tell you was the beauty of such a small town, like Lackton, is that we all know each other inside and out. We know each other's secrets—and because of that we protect one another. If you trust us, and let us trust you, you'll find yourself bein' a part of a family—I can promise you that. That's what small-town life is all about."

I didn't speak. I exhaled, loudly, considering Jasper's words. Was I ready for a new family?

"There's a couple of other things I need to talk with you about," he continued.

"I don't have any plans to leave town, if that's what you're going to ask."

"Well, that's good news, 'cause the first thing I have to talk with you about is that I have an offer you might really like."

I waited for Jasper to explain.

"Ever since you've been playin' catch with Pip, he's improved at our practices and games tremendously. He's still got a long way to go, but he makes a play once in a while, and he's got more confidence. I try to take that momentum and go with it, but he don't interact with me the same way he does with you. Pip is still a little bit afraid of me, even after all the time I've spent with him and his momma. But he's not afraid of you—not one bit."

"What's on your mind, Jasper?"

"I think it would be great for Pip, and probably the rest of my boys, if you'd become my assistant coach. Heck, it'd probably be good for you, too."

I laughed. "You want me to coach baseball?"

"Yes, sir, I do."

"I've never even played baseball. I barely know the rules."

"You think I'm some kinda expert?" Jasper asked. "Heck, most of the time I'm just wingin' it out there."

"We'd make some pair."

"Well, we got Mr. Jack on the staff. His son is our best player, and he knows all the rules and such. Mr. Jack would be the head coach if it weren't for his job bein' so demandin'. He misses just about every practice, but he comes to the games. He and I don't always see eye to eye on philosophy, but I don't give a hoot. It'd be nice to have a feller like you on the staff. I'd betcha you and me think the same."

"Really? How's that?"

"Mr. Jack is all about winnin'. He'd play the same nine boys, every game, and leave the smaller, less talented boys, like Pip, on the bench for the entire season, if I'd let him."

"And you think I'd care less about winning?"

"I know you would. I know you would wanna give *all* of the boys a chance to play. I know you'd wanna see Pip out there, even just a little bit—along with the other kids that ain't exactly all-stars. I believe that's more important to you than winnin' a meaningless baseball game."

I paused a while and thought about Jasper's interpretation of my non-existent coaching style. I'd never played baseball, or any sport. I'd certainly never considered being a coach. I also thought about what I'd been doing with my spare time—next to nothing.

"When's the next practice?" I asked. "Let's do it."

I tried for a high five, but Jasper gave me an odd look and offered a handshake instead.

"There he is—that's my man, right there. We got practice tonight, buddy," Jasper announced.

My smile fell, and a little doubt creeped into my mind.

So soon? Can I actually coach baseball?

Jasper had begun to walk away, but I stopped him. "What's the second thing?"

"Second thing?"

"You said you had a couple of things you needed to talk with me about. The first was about coaching—we talked about that. What's the second thing?"

"Oh yeah, I did say a couple of things, didn't I?" Jasper grinned.

I guessed, based on Jasper's expression, that he was going to ask me what was going on between Lauren and me. I guessed correctly.

"You plannin' on seein' Miss Lauren again, partner?"

I shrugged my shoulders, and gave the impression that I didn't care. I'm not sure I did, at the time.

"I don't really know. I mean, I cried like a baby on our first date. How many relationships have ever gotten past something like that?"

"Come on, man. You know she don't look down on you for that."

"I know. And I should probably talk to her as soon as possible, and thank her for being there for me."

"You're a part of this small town now, Mr. Barrett. You're part of somethin' special. We got your back. We *all* got your back," Jasper repeated.

"I believe that. I really do."

"Good, 'cause it's true. Now don't you be afraid to find Miss Lauren, and ask her out for a do-over. She's a fine woman. And you two are made for each other."

"You're the second person to tell me that."

"That's 'cause it's true, my friend," Jasper insisted. "I'm gonna leave you with that. I'll see you tonight at seven o'clock—at the ballfield. You know where that is, right?"

"Oh yeah, I know where that is. See you there, Jasper."

I stayed a moment longer, at my table, and considered the things Jasper and I had talked about. Coaching seemed a little out of my comfort zone, but it excited me. And I needed something fun to do with my spare time.

Being part of a small-town network of people who cared about me made me feel pretty good. It was certainly something I'd never experienced in Chicago—the concept seemed impossible.

Thinking of the discussion about seeing Miss Lauren again, on an actual date, made me get up and walk back to my apartment. I clearly felt an attraction to her, and she seemed to feel something, too. But I'd never even considered dating anyone other than Charlotte since I was twelve years old.

I don't think I'm ready for that.

Chapter 12

I arrived at practice a few minutes early and sat on one of the picnic tables that served as dugouts on each side of the field. Most of the kids were already there, and Jasper was talking to some of the parents a few yards behind the home plate backstop. I decided to take advantage of the moment and observe the kids to see what kind of group we had.

After the start time of practice had come, and then gone, I looked around for Jasper and found him still chatting—this time, with a different set of parents.

Are we going to get started soon?

Pip had told me that despite having the league's best pitcher, and overall best player, the team was winless in their first three games—and the scores weren't close. Based on the start of my first practice with the team, I developed a theory for why. I even began to suspect we'd finish the season without a single win.

The kids were completely disorganized and definitely not focused on baseball. Most of them were doing their own thing in their own groups. Some were playing catch with each other, which was promising, while others were sitting in the infield grass talking about video games. Pip was sitting alone in the outfield staring out into space, like I'd seen him do many times at Rolling Meadows.

Besides a few kids playing catch, there was one player who seemed to be putting in actual work. It was the same tall, lanky kid who had kicked me and Pip off the field a few weeks prior. He was firing lasers from the pitcher's mound to a catcher who had to stop and shake his hand several times after the ball had popped loudly into his mitt.

I couldn't wait any longer, so I decided it was a good idea to start by introducing myself to the player out on the mound throwing pitches. I correctly assumed he was the player Pip had mentioned—the best pitcher and overall best player in the league. By observing how the other kids behaved around him, I'd determined he was the most popular and respected kid out there.

"That's one heck of a fastball. It's nice to meet you, I'm Coach Barrett."

"Excuse me, *Barrett*. I was about to go into my windup and throw a curveball."

I didn't know much about baseball, but I knew ten-year-old kids shouldn't be throwing curveballs.

"Curveball? How old are you? We don't throw curveballs at the Little League minor level, do we?"

"I do," he replied. "Well, I would—if you'd get out of my way."

"What's your name, young man?"

"That's Nolan," Pip replied. He'd finally noticed I was there, and came over to say hello. "And he's only supposed to throw fastballs and changeups."

"No one asked you, Center Bench. Why don't you go back to sleep in the outfield?" Nolan added.

Pip just looked at me and smiled.

I was about to address Nolan's rude comments to Pip, but he continued before I could. "We already have a coach. We already have an assistant coach, too—my dad, Coach Jack. Why are you even here, exactly?"

"I'm here to help the team," I replied.

Jasper's whistle had drowned out the sound of laughter from most of the players, who'd come over to watch Nolan insult Pip and the new assistant coach.

"Gather 'round boys. Come on over here and meet Coach Barrett," Jasper yelled.

"And Nolan, I don't wanna hear about you tossin' anymore curveballs, son. You throw heaters and you throw changeups. Save those curveballs for when your arm is strong enough."

"My dad says it's okay," Nolan protested.

"Your daddy's not the head coach, boy. And if I see one more curveball in a game, I'm gonna put you on the bench. You hear me? I don't care what your father says 'bout it."

Jasper blew his whistle again, and the team finally came together to start practice—twenty minutes late.

Day one had been a rude awakening for me, which made me question whether I'd be coming back to another practice. I was determined to be there for Pip, so I decided to hang in there and work to improve the things I believed needed the most attention.

Eventually, I helped to develop more of a normal routine. I would arrive early and get all of the kids started on time by lining them into two rows. They stretched, and then played catch, until Jasper came over to begin drills.

Well, all of the kids except for Nolan and our catcher. They stretched with us, but then they worked on Nolan's pitching while the rest of the team played catch.

"The kids are starting to like you," Pip declared at one of our practices. "Most of them wanted to switch teams, because they think Jasper wastes too much time gabbing with parents."

"I told you I'd work on making some new friends. How about you?" I asked. "Are you ready to try and make a few friends? There's plenty of good kids here."

Pip looked at the ground and slid his foot over the sand beneath his feet.

"I know it's hard, Pip. Making friends can be scary for anyone. But once these kids get to know you, they're all going to want to be your friend."

Pip took a deep breath and looked me in the eyes. "I'll try. And I'm going to start with Nolan."

Geez, kid. Are you sure about that?

I looked over at Nolan, who was throwing forbidden curveballs, again. "Well, maybe you should start with…"

Jasper's whistle stopped our conversation short.

From that moment on, Pip was the most focused player at practice. He seemed to be studying the other kids, and at times he'd even offer them pointers on their game—which weren't always received well.

On the day before one of our games, at the end of practice, Jasper and I watched as Pip approached Nolan, who was still on the mound throwing pitches.

I started to go out to intervene, but Jasper stopped me. "No, watch this. He told me he was gonna mention somethin' to Nolan that'd help him with his pitchin'. I wanna see what happens."

"That jerk of a kid is going to tell Pip to go pound sand—or do something worse."

"Give him a chance," Jasper insisted.

We couldn't hear what the boys were saying, at first, but Nolan started to laugh, loudly. "No way! Get out of here with that!" Nolan shouted.

"Seriously," Pip replied, and then he looked over at me and Jasper. "Coach, come over here and watch this," Pip requested.

We walked onto the infield and stopped by the pitcher's mound.

Pip stepped back to give Nolan some room. "Okay, Nolan, throw three changeups, and three fastballs. In any order you want. Trust me, you have a tell."

Pip had suggested to Nolan that he made a subtle glance to the left, at the end of his windup, every time he was about to throw a changeup.

Even if it were true, most of the kids at our level couldn't touch Nolan's pitching. However, if Nolan took that type of habit with him to the next level, it would be trouble.

The whole team gathered to watch Nolan throw six pitches.

"Son of a gun, Pip is right!" Coach Jasper declared.

"You've gotta be kidding me," Nolan said in frustration. "I've been doing that all season?"

"Well, it's okay, Nolan. You're still the best pitcher in the league," Pip offered. "But if you can fix that tell, you're going to be the best pitcher next year, too."

Nolan's face turned red, but he didn't appear to be angry. He'd actually appeared to be embarrassed—like he'd been humbled. For the first time in his young life, the great Nolan Pickett was humbled on the baseball field. But not by a better player. Nolan Pickett was humbled by a kid who'd spent nearly his entire baseball career on the bench.

The team stood by, watching, with their mouths open—astounded. I heard one of the kids tell another about the things Pip was saying to them about corrections they could make in their game.

"Maybe I shoulda listened to him."

Nolan threw a few more pitches, and eventually was able to throw a changeup without the tell. He took off his glove and walked off the mound toward Pip.

I began to move closer to the boys, but Jasper stopped me, again. "Let 'em work it out."

Pip smiled as Nolan approached him, with the blank stare of a gunfighter from the Old West.

Nolan got up close and reached out his arm to Pip, and the boys shook hands. "Nice work, Center…"

He paused and looked around at the entire team. He waited until they were all paying attention, and then returned his gaze toward Pip. "Nice work, Pip. Thank you."

Jasper's face lit up, and he looked at me with what I'd swear was the first smile I'd ever seen on his face. Jasper was elated.

"You see that? Somethin' that simple could be all we need to start changin' things for this team. They just gotta trust one another."

Jasper turned his focus to the rest of the team. "And now, boys, let's build on this moment. Let's come together. How 'bout we start with tomorrow's game and turn this season around?"

Chapter 13

O n Nolan Pickett's eleventh birthday, his mother brought treats to practice for all of the kids on the team. So, we ended practice early, after our typical late start, and the kids gathered around one of the picnic tables that served as dugouts and ate cupcakes.

I think the team put in about ten minutes of actual practice time, but we were on a winning streak so no one seemed to mind.

After Pip had helped Nolan with his pitching tell, the team responded as Coach Jasper had hoped they would and came together. We'd won three straight games, and the playoffs were only a few weeks away.

In our league, all six of the minors teams made the playoffs, so wins and losses didn't matter that much—at least not to a coach like Jasper. The thing that mattered most to him was improving the team, leading into the playoffs, so we could make a decent run at a championship. Still, it obviously felt much better to win than lose.

Though eliminating Nolan Pickett's tell didn't make that much of a difference at our level, he seemed to elevate his game. He was pitching, hitting, and behaving better than he'd been all season.

You'd think a team with a dominant player like that would easily win all of their games, but with restrictions on pitch counts within a single game, and required rest time between days a player pitched, we couldn't rely on just one super-star pitcher—even when our super-star pitcher could also hit the ball better than most of the kids in our league. Baseball is a team sport and winning requires an entire team to play well.

Our team had received its much needed spark when Nolan's general attitude had changed and he became more of a team player. The positive energy seemed to catch on with the rest of the kids. They played better and they had a lot more fun. I believed we ultimately had Pip to thank for that.

Something remarkable also happened while the kids ate Nolan's birthday cupcakes at our practice.

Most of the kids would typically give Nolan a wide berth, out of either respect or fear. As he sat at the picnic table to eat his treat there was plenty of room on both sides of him.

When everyone seemed settled into a spot, sitting on the bench or standing nearby, Nolan looked around and called out, "Where's Pip? Hey, Pip, come sit next to me."

The simple, kind gesture put a smile on Pip's face that was so bright it nearly brought me to tears. Our team was transitioning into something special, even if most hadn't noticed, and our star player was developing into a star human being.

Though Pip's performance had also improved, along with the rest of the team, he still hadn't touched the ball with his bat during a game.

In fact, every time Pip had an opportunity to bat, which wasn't very often, Coach Jack had convinced Coach Jasper to tell him not to swing—ever. Pip's only hope for reaching base would be four balls and a walk.

During one of our days off from the team, I decided to take Pip to the field to see if we could work on his hitting. I wanted to see him swing his bat.

When we had reached the end of the trail between Rolling Meadows and the ballfield, Pip noticed Nolan and a few other kids from the team there, hanging around on one of the picnic tables.

"Maybe we should go and play in the grass back home."

"No way, Pip. We're done letting these guys push us around. They're not even using the field."

Pip's eyes widened, and he gazed at his feet as we approached the infield.

One of the kids began shouting, "Hey, Center Bench, who said you could come out here and use our field?"

The boy was immediately given a swift backhand to the arm by Nolan, and he shrieked in pain.

Nolan stood up and turned to his whimpering friend and to the other kids who were sitting on the picnic table.

"Pip is our teammate," he declared, with authority. Then he turned and looked toward Pip and me. "And it looks like he's here to work on his game. Would y'all like some help?"

Pip smiled and answered, "Yes, please. We're gonna work on my hitting!"

"Let's do it," Nolan answered back. "I'll throw you some soft pitches."

Nolan turned to the other kids and demanded, "The rest of y'all get behind me and field the balls."

He then turned to me, "Coach, would you mind playing catcher?"

"Of course," I answered. "Thank you, Nolan. This is really kind of you," I added.

Nolan must have thrown a hundred slow pitches, in between pausing and offering patient instruction to Pip, but he never got upset, he never changed his positive tone, and he never stopped giving advice.

One-by-one, we lost our fielders, who claimed they had to go home for dinner or any other excuse they could think of. They were more likely leaving due to boredom because they hadn't had anything to do since Pip hadn't made contact with any of the meatballs Nolan was tossing to him.

Finally, long after everyone else had gone home, and only the three of us remained at the ballpark, Nolan walked off the pitcher's mound and made his way toward us at home plate.

"Those were some good cuts, Pip. You're gonna make contact soon enough. Don't you give up, ya hear me? I know you can hit one."

I nodded in agreement, "Thanks again, Nolan. We really do appreciate your help."

"I'll see y'all at practice," Nolan added, and then he left us.

I waited for Nolan to get far enough away, so he couldn't hear me, and then I asked Pip, "What the heck happened to that guy? He's like a brand new kid, right?"

"He's starting to get it."

"Get it? Get what? He went from being a bully to being a great person. All of that, just because you helped him with his pitching?"

"He's going to be a great baseball player someday. That's his future, and it doesn't matter how many games his team in Lackton Youth Baseball wins. He knows that now."

"So it's all about him no longer caring about wining? I don't understand what you mean by that, Pip."

"Well, being angry at your team all the time, because it's full of kids with less than half of your talent, is a terrible way to spend your summer. And a plastic trophy won't do much for you either, except collect dust."

"That's true," I agreed. "But, what do you think caused him to change?" I asked. And then I realized that I was asking a ten-year-old a deep philosophical question, and I chuckled.

"He's always been a great person, he just needed to be reminded that there are great people around him—

even if they stink at baseball and he loses all his games. I think we helped him realize that and now the real Nolan is showing up."

This kid never ceases to amaze me.

"Now all we need to do is remind his father of that," I joked.

"Yeah, it may be too late for Coach Jack."

"There's my handsome little man!" Lauren shouted from the opening of the trail. "You gonna come home at some point tonight, and join us for dinner?"

I hadn't spoken to Lauren since our evening together at Cattleman's. I still owed her a thank you, or possibly an apology. I'd been avoiding her, afraid to offer either.

I stared at her in silence, like a deer, frozen by fear from the glare of oncoming headlights, as she approached us from the woods. Even in her nursing scrubs, with her long, dark hair pulled back in a ponytail, and sneakers on her feet, she was stunning.

"You still there, Mr. Barrett?" Pip asked. He nudged at my hip to bring me back, and smiled at me when I finally looked at him.

"Yeah, I was just zoned out. Let's head home before you get into trouble."

"You like her, don't you?"

"Well, I like most people."

"You especially like Aunt Lauren though."

I continued playing coy. "I have no reason to dislike her. She's nice," I added.

"She's pretty hot, too, and I think she likes you back. So what are you gonna do about it?"

I turned quickly to Pip and raised my eyebrows. "She's what, now?" I asked. "She's hot? That's your aunt you're speaking about, buddy."

Pip laughed. "Well, she's not *really* my aunt. She's just my mom's best friend. She's done a lot for us, so she's kind of an honorary aunt to me."

"Uh huh, well I think she's too old for you."

"I don't think about her like that, I just wanted to confirm that you did. And, obviously, you do."

Do I? I'm still not sure I'm ready for that.

Lauren had made it to where we were talking. "Hello, gentlemen. Pip, you ready to head home?"

"I'll see you there, Aunt Lauren. You two enjoy your alone time," he shouted, and then he ran toward the trail ahead of us, giggling.

"He's such an amazing kid," I said, as we slowly made our way into the woods.

"He sure is. He's one of a kind."

After a few moments of awkward silence, I finally spoke up. "Listen, about that night, at the bar," I started.

"It's okay, you don't need to explain anything."

"I know that," I replied, in relief. "But, I wanted to say thank you. I've needed someone to talk to for a very long time. Thank you for being there."

"It was my pleasure," Lauren replied, and then she stopped walking and grabbed my hand.

"Barrett, you've been through something that most people couldn't even imagine. You shouldn't expect to be okay right away. But hiding away from a painful past isn't a very healthy way to spend the rest of your life."

"I know, and I realized that after our talk. I'm coming around, slowly."

We'd started walking again and I hadn't even realized we were still holding hands when we got to the Rolling Meadows end of the trail.

I gently pulled my hand back, and pointed toward my apartment. "I'm that way."

Lauren pointed toward Pip, who was staring at us with his hands over his mouth. Apparently he'd noticed the hand holding.

"And I'm that way," she gently replied.

I wanted to say more, but I couldn't find the words. I wanted to ask Lauren out to dinner, or something—anything. But I didn't.

"Enjoy your dinner. Goodnight, Lauren," was all I could manage, and I turned and walked home, in agony.

Chapter 14

J asper had called for a coach's meeting prior to our first playoff game to talk strategy. This was the same Coach Jasper who hadn't started a practice on time all season, and who rarely knew the score of any of the games we'd played, neither during nor after the game.

It was exciting though, and I'd enjoyed my time with the team, even if my biggest responsibilities on game days had been counting pitches and filling out a scoresheet, incorrectly—every time.

I showed up early, at Cattleman's, eager to do my part to strategize and help our team win the Lackton Youth Baseball minor's championship.

A championship victory would earn Coach Jasper and me the honor of coaching the all-star game, where we would inevitably be slaughtered by Kipford. The kids on our team had repeatedly joked about that. It was the most logical outcome, regardless of who the coaches would be, based on the history of baseball competition—and just about everything else— between the two towns. Kipford always came out on top.

"Hi, sugar, it's good to have you back," Jasper's sister called out from behind the bar.

I smiled and sat on a stool at a small high-top table across from Jasper, who had arrived even earlier than me.

"Look at that, you're a regular now, I guess. She don't greet just anybody like that. Most folks are lucky if they get a, 'What do you want?' and a growl outta her."

"You hush your mouth, Jasper. He's sweet, so he's my sugar. And he's welcome in here anytime," she added, with a wink in my direction. "Wish I could say any of those things about you, brother."

I did my best to quickly change the subject. I was feeling pretty awkward, considering the last time I'd been at Cattleman's I'd left in tears.

"Do we need to move to a bigger table? There's no room for Jack," I pointed out.

"Coach Jack won't be here. He never shows up to nothin', except games."

The bartender came to our table with two draft pints of beer. "This one's on me, sugar," she said as she put one of the beers in front of me, "and I'll add this one to your overdue tab, Jasper," she added with a half-hearted scowl.

"Thanks, witch," Jasper replied.

"So, what kind of strategy did you have in mind, for the playoffs?" I asked.

"Well, best I can come up with is we do our best to win three games. The top two teams got a bye—we ain't one of them—so we play for a spot in the semi-finals, and then, if we win, it's on to the final. If we win that one, we get a trophy."

"And then, if we win it all, we get to coach the all-star game against Kipford?"

Jasper chuckled. "Don't get ahead of yourself there, Coach Barrett. Let's just play 'em one game at a time."

"Fair enough, but it would great to put together a team and show Kipford what we can do. We get two players from each team, right?"

"If we win the Lackton championship, and that's a big if, we coach the all-star team. Each team sends their two best players, or two players voted on by players and coaches, and the all-star team's coach gets to pick one kid from any team to add. Most of the time, they pick a third player from their own regular-season team."

"I have no idea who our third best player is," I admitted.

"Listen, don't even think about any of that right now. Let's just focus on winnin' our first game."

"Sorry, this is way more exciting than I'd ever imagined."

"Good, I'm glad you feel that way. Now you gotta work on gettin' the kids excited. If they play their best, we got a shot. But only if they play their best."

"So, do we hold out pitching Nolan until the third game? Maybe play him at shortstop for games one and two?"

"We gotta win game one first, and then worry about games two and three, right?"

I nodded in agreement.

"So, he pitches game one, and we see how it all plays out. If we can keep his pitch count low in game one, he should be able to pitch in game three, if we can make it that far without him on the mound in game two."

"That sounds like a plan," I offered with enthusiasm.

Jasper emptied his draft and nodded. I waited for him to lay out the rest of his strategy—he didn't.

"What else do you have in mind?" I asked.

"That's just about all I got," Jasper admitted.

"That's the whole meeting?"

"Yup, I suppose it is."

"You just called a meeting so we could hang out and drink beer, didn't you?"

"Yup, I suppose that's true, too."

I shrugged. It seemed like a fine idea to me. "Well, in that case, do you think your sister will buy me another beer?"

Jasper nearly howled with laughter. "I wouldn't count on that, partner. But you can buy us another round."

I brought another round of drafts to the table and we started a new conversation that had nothing to do with youth baseball.

"So, when are you gonna ask the lovely Miss Lauren out on a real date?" Jasper asked.

I just sighed. It was a good question—one I'd asked myself over and over again, but couldn't answer.

I immediately changed the subject instead. "How about you? When are you going to tell Sheila how you feel about her? I think she likes you."

"I'm not sure it'd be appropriate with me bein' her landlord and all."

I pulled back my head quickly and lifted my arms in the air. There was no way I'd let him get away with that.

"Oh, come on. First of all, you're not actually the landlord, and more importantly, *everyone* knows you're in love with her—including her. And she's great, by the way," I added.

Jasper's expression changed. He leaned toward me with his arms folded in front of him on the high-top table and spoke softly, like he had a secret to tell me. Or maybe it was to hide his fear or insecurity, "You think she'd be interested in a man like me?"

I paused and thought about Jasper's question. Of course she'd be interested in him. Jasper was a good man—Pip loved him, he loved Pip, and I had honestly believed Sheila was just waiting for him to make a move.

"Do you own a nice suit?" I asked.

Jasper furrowed his brow. "I don't even own a not-nice suit. What are you gettin' at?"

"Do you love Sheila? Answer me honestly."

"Yes sir, I suppose I do."

"That's all I needed to hear," I replied. "Are you ready to make a grand gesture for the woman you love?"

"Just what are you getting' at?" Jasper repeated.

"Well, first we're gonna go shopping to get you a suit, and then you're going to work on your waltz."

"I can't afford all that."

"It's on me, my friend. And it'll be worth every penny when you sweep Sheila off her feet."

"Are you 'bout to suggest I show up at Miss Sheila's dance class in a monkey suit? I don't know if I'm up for that."

"Yes, I am, and with flowers—a grand gesture."

If Jasper looked afraid before, he looked positively horrified now.

"It worked wonders for Miss Tammy," I joked. "Where's she been, anyway?"

Jasper's expression of horror didn't change, and he answered without looking me in the eyes. "She moved out. She moved in with that Mason feller she met at Miss Sheila's dance class."

"No kidding? That's great, I'm really happy for her."

Jasper finally looked up at me, "Do you really think somethin' like that could work for me?"

"I do, and it will. I think all you need to do, when it comes to winning Sheila's heart, is make a move. And you may as well make a great move, right? A grand gesture," I repeated.

Jasper grinned, and it was obvious he had something besides just professing his love for Sheila on his mind. "I'll do it, but on one condition."

I knew immediately where he was going, based on his expression.

"I'll get all dressed up, in a fancy suit, ready to dance with Miss Sheila. I'll even bring long-stem roses. And don't you worry about my waltz—I got that one covered," he added with a wink.

Who knew Jasper could dance?

"I'll do all of that, if you make me one simple promise."

"What do want me to do?" I asked, but I already knew the answer.

"Before I show up, wearing my new monkey suit, you gotta ask Miss Lauren out on a real date."

And there it was.

Chapter 15

Our first playoff game was a day away and we had the night off from practice. I'd done my best to get the kids excited, and ready to play hard, like Coach Jasper had requested.

Honestly, I don't think any of them were nearly as excited as I was—except for Nolan Pickett, of course.

I'd discovered something that was pretty obvious while being a part of a youth sports team for the first time in my life. The adults—coaches and parents—experienced far more bliss from wins, and far, far more agony from losses than any of their children, who were actually playing the games, ever did.

While the adults left the field, after a loss, still brooding and complaining amongst the other adults about a bad call, or a blind umpire, or some other horrible injustice, the kids—win or lose—were laughing and playing with teammates and opponents alike, or making plans to have sleepovers, or making plans to get home quickly and meet up with each other online to play video games together.

All of the kids behaved in this manner after every game, except for Pip—and Nolan Pickett, of course.

Pip, who up to that point had struggled to make friends on the team, would blissfully run off the field to the open arms of his mother, Sheila, and tell her every detail about the game she had just watched as they walked home through the trail to Rolling Meadows.

Nolan would eventually join the other kids in whatever plans were being constructed after a game, but before he did he would be required to run sprints for his father if he played poorly or made a mistake on the field. And though I'd failed to spot any mistakes in Nolan's game all season, his father, Coach Jack, had found plenty.

As I sat alone at my table on the lawn, thinking about how our baseball season had progressed, and how much progress I'd made building a new life in Lackton, Oklahoma, I spotted Pip approaching me with an unusual look on his face.

When Pip had reached my table, he was fidgeting with a blue folder that he was carrying and he didn't greet me with his customary smile. He didn't look me in the eyes either, like he had always done while speaking to me. He looked skyward instead, and there was a long pause before he finally spoke his first words. He was clearly nervous about something.

"I have some great news, and I have some not-so-great news," Pip announced.

"Let's start with the great news," I suggested, "and then we can work out the not-so-great news."

"Okay, the great news. Well, remember when you told me that I should show my *Space Lordz* books to someone?"

"I do, and I stand by that—they're excellent."

"Right, well, I shortened one of them up, and Aunt Lauren typed it out on her laptop, and then we submitted it to *Inch Worm Magazine's* Future Writers Contest."

"You did? That's awesome. Good for you, Pip," I added, and then I paused. "So what's the not-so-great news? Did your book not do very well?"

"I won," Pip answered, and then he swallowed hard and his eyes shifted even farther skyward.

"Whoa! That is definitely not, not-so-great news. Are you kidding me? That's incredibly great news."

"I mean, I'm excited about winning the contest, but the prize isn't so great."

"How is that possible? You won, buddy!"

"I won a two-week stay at a writer's camp, in Texas."

"I'm still not seeing a problem. What's wrong? You love writing," I reassured. "Does this mean you won't be able to play baseball in the playoffs?" I asked.

"No, the camp doesn't start until two weeks after baseball season is over. And my mom is making me go, but I won't know anyone there—no one at all. I won't have any friends, or anyone to talk to."

I took a deep breath and nodded. The thought of making new friends wasn't just difficult for Pip—it was paralyzing. I could see tears building up in his eyes as he considered being in a strange place, with strange people, for two whole weeks.

"Would it help if I drove you there? And if we promised to exchange letters every day while you were gone?"

Pip's eyes widened, and he looked at me with a hint of hope. "Do you think the people at the camp would let us do that?" he asked.

"I'm sure if your mom talked to the counselors, or teachers, or whoever's in change, they'd let it slide."

Though Pip's expression had changed from one of anguish to one of hope, a tear had escaped and rolled down one of his cheeks.

"Mr. Barrett," he said softly.

"Yeah? What is it, buddy?" I asked.

"You're a really good friend."

Chapter 16

At the start of all of our regular season games, I'd made it a habit to wait for Coach Jack to settle into a spot on the bench, or whatever patch of grass he'd be pacing on during the game, before choosing a spot for myself—so I could be as far away from him as possible.

I'd especially enjoyed the half innings when our team was batting, because Jack was our third base coach and he was even farther away. This made it less likely for someone to confuse which coach at our bench was complaining or swearing about nearly every call—bad or not—that went against our team.

Coach Jasper and I took turns coaching our runners from first base, but Jasper had informed me that during the playoffs he'd be handling that responsibility full-time. This left me on the bench, keeping a close watch on pitch counts for both our team and our opponent's team for the duration of the playoffs.

I was thankful for Jasper's decision, because I'd always been a little too conservative, in Coach Jack's opinion, when it came to having kids steal second base. I was looking forward to not being yelled at from third base during the playoffs.

My most critical responsibility during our first playoff game, was to tell Coach Jasper when Nolan Pickett had reached forty pitches. Our goal was to keep him under fifty so he'd only be required to rest his arm two days and be eligible to pitch in our third game—if we were lucky enough to win game two and reach the third game, which happened to be the league championship game.

I had handled my pitch-counting duties like a seasoned veteran, and we pulled Nolan off the mound before he'd reached fifty pitches, with just two innings left to play. Nolan did his job, too, by not allowing a single runner to cross home plate. The only problem was, we hadn't scored any runs either.

A combination of two boys pitched for our team for the rest of the game. Their efforts helped us get to the bottom of the last inning with the score tied at two runs apiece—and our team was up to bat. We just needed one run to win the game.

With a runner at first, and two outs, I sent Pip to the plate to take his first and only at bat of the game. Until then, he'd spent the afternoon on the bench.

Coach Jasper had promised the kids, and parents, that every kid would get at least one chance to bat in every game—no exceptions. So, I did what I'd believed Coach Jasper would do, and I sent Pip out to bat.

"Time out!" yelled Coach Jack from his coaching spot near third base.

Jack made his way toward me, at the picnic table-dugout, and Jasper came over from his spot near first base.

"What the hell do you think you're doing?" Jack asked. "This is the playoffs. That kid doesn't leave the bench."

"Now hold on just one minute, Jack, the rule is, every kid has to get at least one at bat per game," Jasper explained.

"This isn't officially Little League Baseball, Coach," Jack snapped back. "No one cares about that rule in Lackton Youth Baseball."

"I care," Jasper insisted. "Coach Barrett made the right call. Pip gets his at bat. Now go on back over to third, and let's see if we can get this win—the right way."

Jack looked at me like I'd just insulted his entire way of life and shook his head. He was furious, but he knew better than to try to win an argument with Jasper.

He started to make his way back to third base, but then he turned and walked over to home plate and had a quick and quiet conversation with Pip.

I'd assumed he'd told Pip what he always told Pip when it was his turn to bat—"Don't you swing that bat. Just crouch down low, and hope he walks you!"—but I didn't hear any of their conversation.

After the quick talk with Coach Jack, Pip's smile was gone, and he stepped out of the batter's box and looked toward me. I started to walk onto the field toward him, but the umpire stopped me.

"Play ball!" shouted the umpire.

Pip stepped back up to the plate and swallowed hard.

The first pitch was a strike, and Pip nearly fell as he backed away from the fastball. The kid on the mound threw harder than anyone in our league—except for Nolan Pickett.

"Come on, Pip. Just like we talked about," Coach Jack shouted.

What is he up to?

"Strike two!" shouted the umpire, after a second fastball flew by Pip, nearly hitting his elbow as it came in tight, but over the corner of the plate.

"Come on now, Pip. Don't be scared. Just like I told you," Coach Jack shouted.

Oh no. Don't tell me…

"AHHH!" Pip screamed in pain, and then he flopped to the ground right on top of home plate. He'd leaned in, just slightly, but enough to get in the way of the oncoming third pitch, which hit him, hard, just below his shoulder.

I looked over at Jack and he was clapping from his coaching spot near third base. He'd actually told Pip to lean into a fastball and take one for the team!

Jasper and I ran to Pip, who was laying on the ground near home plate, holding his arm, crying.

"It's alright, son, it's alright—I got you," Jasper added as he rubbed Pip's arm. And then he helped the crying boy to his feet.

"I did it," Pip announced, as tears continued to fall down his cheeks. "I got us another base runner. I didn't give up the last out and cost us the game."

Jasper's expression went blank, and he looked over at Jack, who was still smiling and clapping. I could feel Jasper's anger as his face turned bright red. He turned, ready to make his way toward Jack, like a bull who'd spotted the matador waving a bright cape to draw him in for the final, and fatal, sabre strike.

"Coach Barret?" Jasper asked, calmly—eerily.

"Yes, Coach?" I replied.

"Please tend to Pip, and have someone take over for him. Tell the umpire you're putting in a pinch runner."

"Yes, Coach," I replied, and then I helped Pip over to the bench.

The umpire put a hand on Jasper's shoulder, but quickly pulled it away after Jasper snapped back at him with a look of fierce determination.

"Take your time, Coach," the umpire said.

Coach Jack's smile faded and his claps slowed to a stop as Coach Jasper made his way toward him.

"I'm only gonna ask one time, Jack, and you better not say a single word back."

"What are you talking about, coach? We're in great shape. One hit and we win the game."

"Not one more word," Jasper repeated. "Now, please get off the field and head on home. You're not welcome on my team no more, and I don't wanna see you around my boys no more, either."

Jack started to object, but before he could get a word out, Jasper's eyes widened, and he quickly changed his mind and did as the head coach had requested.

Jack made his way to the bench, tugged Nolan's arm, and then father and son walked to their car and drove away. No one in the stands said a word the entire time—the silence was deafening.

"Play ball!" the umpire shouted.

Coach Jasper pointed to me, and then to first, indicating he wanted me to coach first base as he made his way over to Jack's spot at third.

I could hear one of the boys on the bench complain to another boy, "We're gonna get creamed without Nolan on the team."

If we manage to win this game, we are gonna get creamed tomorrow, without Nolan.

With a little luck on our side, the next kid at bat got a base hit, and we won our first playoff game. But no one was in the mood to celebrate.

Chapter 17

W e'd not only lost our best player, but we had the dubious honor of facing the number one team in the league for game two of the playoffs. And since our second round opponent had a bye in the first round, all of their pitchers were fully rested and ready to play.

Watching Nolan Pickett being dragged away from the dugout the night before had been a morale killer for our team, and whatever magic we'd created leading up to that moment was dragged away with him.

Pregame warmups were quiet, and none of the kids looked like they even wanted to play.

"Let's pick our heads up, boys, we got a game to play," Jasper shouted as he made his way onto the field.

"We're down two kids, coach," I declared. "Pip's not here yet, and, well, you know about Nolan."

"Where the heck is Pip?" Jasper asked.

I shrugged.

"Hey coach, look who I found!" Pip shouted as he made his way out of the trailhead with his mother, Aunt Lauren, and a beaming Nolan Pickett.

"Are y'all ready to take this game, and earn our spot in the championship, or what? Let's go!" Nolan roared as he made his way onto the field to join warmups.

Nolan exchanged high fives and smiles with every one of his teammates. In that brief moment, we'd gone from a group of lambs, ripe for slaughter, to a pride of lions, ready to hunt for victory.

I'd noticed Pip had stopped at the dugout and took a seat when Nolan came out on the field. He wasn't dressed for baseball, and his arm was wrapped up in some sort of a homemade sling, so I made my way over to talk with him.

"She didn't want to, but I made my mom drive me over to Nolan's house so we could talk to his mother. We convinced her to let Nolan play. To be honest, it really wasn't that hard at all," Pip declared. "I think Nolan's mom is pretty mad at Coach Jack."

I laughed, and nodded. "I suppose she could be, buddy."

"Yeah, I know, right?" Pip acknowledged the obvious.

I changed my demeanor and pointed at Pip's make-shift sling. "What's up with your arm, is that a sling? Why aren't you dressed for the game?"

"My arm's still sore from taking one for the team last night. I think I need to sit out for a while."

"Pip, no one's ever going to ask you to do anything like that again. Are you sure you don't want to play? You have time to run home and get your uniform on."

"No, I'm good. If it's alright, I'll just sit here and cheer the team on."

"Of course it's alright, but you're welcome to join us if you change your mind."

Warmups were ending, and the rest of the team had begun to join us at the bench.

"Coach Jasper, would it be okay if I say a few things, before the game?" Nolan asked.

"That sounds like a great idea, son. Why don't you give the pregame speech? It's your team, Nolan."

Nolan took a few steps away from the bench, cleared his throat, and turned to address the team.

Everyone stopped what they were doing and gave him their full attention.

Jasper looked at me, and winked. He was tickled by the moment, and he looked on at his team, proudly, with his arms crossed, happy to give Nolan the floor.

"So, guys, I just wanted to say a few things," Nolan started. "This team didn't do so good at the start of the season—we really didn't have much of team at all. Also, I was rude to most of you, and I'm sorry for that. For some reason I believed I was better than the team."

"You are better, Nolan," a boy interrupted. "You're the best player in the league. My dad says you're gonna be pro ballplayer someday."

All of the other kids nodded in agreement.

"That stuff doesn't matter right now," Nolan insisted. "It's not even about that. We're playing this game, today, because we came together as a team. And I couldn't have got us here by myself. I couldn't have won a single game without all of you."

Nolan walked over to Pip and put a hand on his good arm. "And this whole team couldn't have gotten here without Pip. Heck, y'all, I wouldn't even be here right now if it wasn't for Pip."

The boys started chattering, and one of them shouted, "Let's hear it for Pip!"

Nolan quickly brought them back to attention. "I'm not pitching today, but it doesn't matter. We have my bat, we have y'alls' skills, and, today, we all have Pip's heart. Now let's go out there and win this game!"

The players all stood and surrounded Nolan, shouting and jumping.

We might actually win this game.

Chapter 18

Nolan Pickett had played the best game of his very young baseball career in game two of our playoff run. Without his father there to constantly shout at him, at the umpire, at the coach on the opposing team, at the coach on *our* team, or at anyone else who he would've deemed to have earned his ire, Nolan was in complete command of his game.

The young man, who played the entire game at shortstop, had a hit at every at bat—with two home runs. The rest of the kids played their hearts out, and we'd managed to win a slugfest of a game by a score of thirteen to eleven.

When the dust finally settled after the game we all cheered for Nolan, and the cheers grew even louder when coach Jasper had managed to retrieve one of his home run balls from the woods. Coach Jasper wrote the date and Nolan's name on the ball, and presented it to our star player as a keepsake.

We had the next night off, and then the championship game the next day, with our ace officially rested and ready to pitch us to victory.

In the championship game, Nolan proved to be up for the task, which surprised no one. He pitched a complete-game shutout. He also belted a solo home run in the first inning, which proved to be the game winner of a three to zero win.

Pip, who didn't play because he still hadn't removed the make-shift sling from his arm, tried to find Nolan's home run ball in the woods, but failed. When he'd returned empty-handed from his hunt, he declared the ball must still be flying—all the way to Mexico.

Sheila and Lauren, along with several of the other parents, had prepared a pizza party, complete with congratulatory cake and ice cream. The proud parents had everything prepared and waiting for the team to help cap off the championship win—right there at the ballfield.

Before Coach Jasper excused us, however, he called a quick team meeting out in centerfield, away from anyone who wasn't actually part of the team. We had some unfinished business to discuss before we could celebrate our unexpected victory.

"First off, I wanna tell y'all how proud I am to be your coach," Jasper began. He had tears in his eyes.

"We came together as a team this season, and we done it right, too, all the way through 'till the end. Great job, guys. Let's hear it one more time!" Coach Jasper added, and the team followed with shouts and cheers.

"I put this off as long as I could, 'cause I didn't want any unnecessary distractions, but we need to have a vote and pick all-stars for the game next weekend against Kipford."

"Coach, we get three, right?" Nolan asked.

"We get two, actually, and then since y'all won the championship, that means I get to coach the all-star team, and pick any player I want, from the entire league," Jasper corrected.

"Well, you're obviously gonna pick one of our players, right?"

Jasper smiled and shrugged, causing the team to laugh. "I mean, I dunno. Wasn't I supposed to be payin' attention to the kids on the other teams?"

"You barely paid any attention to us!" one of the players shouted, and the rest of the team erupted with more laughter.

"Seriously though, I called y'all over here 'cause I want you to decide. I wanna team vote, first on our two all-stars, and then on another player—any player in the league, that you want to add to the all-star team."

"Nolan!" shouted one of the players, and then every kid on the team echoed the first vote.

"Right, so Nolan is our first player on the all-star team. Now, y'all pick another," Jasper added.

A few names were spoken aloud, and then the team voted on one of our other pitchers, who had closed out game one and started game two of our playoff run. He was a solid choice.

"Alright, I'm good with that one too, congratulations boys," Jasper said, and then he shook hands with our two elected all-stars.

"Coach Jasper, before we vote on that third player, I'd like to make a suggestion to the team," Nolan requested.

"I think you've earned that right, son. Who'd you have in mind?"

The team had been sitting in a circle around me and Coach Jasper, and Nolan stood up and joined us in the center to address the team with his suggestion.

"Before y'all laugh me off the field, let me tell you why I think this kid should be our third all-star," Nolan insisted.

None of the kids interrupted, and I would have been shocked if any of them dared to disobey Nolan.

He continued, "He helped me become a better pitcher, I promise you that, and he also helped me realize I was bein' a jackass."

The kids giggled, a little, but none were brave enough to let Nolan see them laughing.

"And Casey, remember when you was having trouble with all them popups? He was the one who told Coach Barrett to tell you to stop swinging your bat upward, tryin' to hit balls over the fence. You got a lotta nice hits after that, remember?"

"I remember Coach Barrett tellin' me that, but who told him to?" Casey asked.

All of the kids turned their heads to look at me, but I wasn't about to reveal my source. I was actually getting choked up, because I knew who Nolan was suggesting, and the notion had positively touched my heart.

"I've been watchin' him, and I think he's helped just about all of us, at one time or another, over the season.

Y'all should know darn well who I'm talking about, now" Nolan added.

"You don't mean Center Bench, do you, Nolan?" a player asked.

Everyone quickly turned and looked at Pip, who was sitting there with his perpetual smile. "I don't know who the heck he's talking about," Pip admitted.

"Y'all cut it out with that Center Bench stuff," Nolan demanded. "His name is Pippen Hammond—and he's my friend."

"Sorry, Pip," replied the boy who'd just called him Center Bench.

"It's alright. I kinda like being on the bench. You can call me Center Bench all you want, guys."

The team responded with laughter, and then something amazing happened. The players started chattering among themselves—one by one, they told stories about how Pip had helped them with some fundamental part of their game, or how he had done something nice to lift their spirits at practice. They were actually beginning to agree with Nolan, and appeared ready to vote Pip into the all-star game.

"Nolan, son, go ahead and make your official suggestion for our third all-star. We got a victory party over there waitin' for us," Coach Jasper pointed out.

"I pick Center Bench!" Nolan shouted.

"Center Bench! Center Bench! Center Bench!" most of the team chanted.

"But, wait a minute," one of the kids interrupted, "He's hurt. He's still got a sling over his arm—look at it."

"This thing?" Pip asked. "I think my arm is feeling much better now," he declared, and then he tossed the sling out into center field. "I'm ready to play, guys!"

The entire team applauded the gesture from Pip, and the chant continued—the vote for the third all-star was unanimous.

"Center Bench! Center Bench! Center Bench!"

Chapter 19

L auren had come to all of our playoff games, and we'd exchanged glances and smiles but I'd never approached her.

She was there after the championship game, handing out pizza to hungry kids, and Jasper caught me staring at her, which I admittedly did—a lot.

"When are you gonna come to your senses and ask that pretty lady, right there, out on a date? I sure hope it's before some lesser man beats you to it."

"What about you? Have you gone to Sheila's dance class yet? Remember, *the grand gesture*? We picked out the perfect suit for it."

"We ain't talkin' about me and Sheila right now. And don't you worry about that. It's all happenin', in due time—I got it figured out," Jasper promised. "But you were supposed to take Miss Lauren out on the town, man. What's your plan, Mr. Barrett?"

I didn't answer. I didn't have a plan. I just kept staring at Lauren while she smiled and handed out slices of pizza.

She stopped for a moment and caught me looking at her.

I just smiled and waved, she smiled back, and then she motioned me to come over to her.

"Are you coaches going to eat some of this pizza? It's going pretty fast—I'm worried that I may not have bought enough food."

"I'll be fine. Let the kids have at it—they earned it."

"Are you sure? I can save you a couple slices, if you want me to."

"How about you and I have something a little more upscale than pizza?" I asked.

Lauren didn't quite understand the question, at first, and gave me a puzzled look. "We have pizza, cake, and ice cream. That's all we have on the menu, I'm afraid."

I smiled, and tried again. "I was thinking maybe you and I could pass on the pizza, and go out to dinner later—if you're free, of course. I mean, if you'd want to go out with me."

Lauren closed her eyes and laughed at herself for not picking up on the line. "I'm free tonight. Are you asking me out on a date, Coach Barrett?"

A few of the kids heard Lauren's question, and there were whispers and pointing. Pip had heard too, and smiled at me, waiting for me to answer his Aunt Lauren's question.

"I am, indeed, Miss Lauren, asking you out on a date," I replied, loudly.

The rest of the kids heard that time, and no one made a sound. Everyone shifted their focus toward Lauren, and we all eagerly awaited her response.

"I'd love to."

I exhaled, and the kids laughed. Nolan actually came over and patted me on the back. "Nice work, Coach Barrett. Not the greatest execution, but excellent results."

Are we done here yet?

Lauren actually walked me home from the ballfield and we finalized our dinner plans on the way. She gave me her address, which was in Kipford, and a surprise peck on the lips, before heading home to get ready for our night out.

The simple gesture hit me like a freight train, and I smiled, awkwardly. "I'll pick you up in about two hours?" was all I could manage to say.

"Looking forward to it."

Apparently it was enough.

I'd picked the perfect spot to take Lauren on our date weeks before actually having the nerve to ask her if she'd go. Daniel Timothy's in Kipford was the clear first choice for fine dining in our little corner of Oklahoma—and she said she loved the place when I offered it as an option.

Now I just had to keep my nerves in check and hope everything else went as smoothly. I hadn't been on a date with anyone except Charlotte since, well, since never.

Am I actually going to do this?

Charlotte and I had actually talked about that very moment, many years before she was gone. We'd both promised that if one of us should pass away, the other should find someone else and live the rest of their life to the fullest. Of course, that promise was far easier to make than it was to live up to.

"She would want you to be happy," I said to myself in the mirror while preparing for the evening. "She does want you to be happy, and so does David."

Saying my son's name aloud, even to myself, sent a painful shock through my body.

My beautiful David.

I fought back the tears and repeated myself. "They both want you to be happy. You deserve to be happy.

Lauren is a terrific person—Charlotte and David would love her."

I stayed there, in front of the mirror, until I could say those words aloud, without wanting to cry.

My mood improved on the drive to Lauren's apartment, and I couldn't help but laugh at the vehicle I was driving.

I thought out loud. "I'm showing up at a beautiful woman's apartment, to take her out to a four-star restaurant—five-star if you consider our other options—and this old beater is the best I could do?"

It was the first time since moving to Lackton that I'd ever felt odd about my pickup. And the thought of bringing Lauren to my apartment, on that night, or any future night, made me shudder.

"I think I may be ready for some changes," I declared.

I rang the bell to Lauren's apartment, and when she greeted me I froze. It wasn't because I was having second thoughts—I wasn't. It was because Lauren was far more stunning than any other time I'd seen her.

She had her long, dark hair down and a short, black form-fitting dress over her slender frame.

"You look amazing," I finally managed to say.

My look of astonishment made Lauren blush. "You look pretty sharp yourself."

"Your chariot awaits, my lady" I declared. "I'm sorry, but the best I could do was this old pickup."

"It'll do nicely. This is Oklahoma, after all."

"I'm considering trading her in. Maybe getting something a little more comfortable."

"Well, I love her. She's a classic beauty."

Indeed, she is. Are we still talking about the truck?

The evening, the company, the dress, and the atmosphere at Daniel Timothy's were absolutely perfect. I didn't feel any of the nerves I'd been worried about.

"It's not Cattleman's, but it'll do," I joked.

"If you play this right, we'll end up doing shots at Cattleman's, later."

"Can't wait."

We never made it to Cattleman's that night, but we both definitely played it right. The conversation was easy and fun. I felt alive for the first time in two years. I felt like I had something to look forward to— something to strive for. I felt amazing.

Charlotte was with me the entire night, but not to hold me back or make me feel guilty. She was there encouraging me. She was telling me to enjoy myself—it was clear to me. My family was happy for me.

If I had to fight back any tears that night, they were tears of joy, not tears of pain.

"I think I'm going to be okay," I accidentally said out loud.

Lauren didn't ask me what I meant. She just smiled and nodded, knowingly. "I think so, too."

This is perfect. She's perfect.

I changed the subject, before things got uncomfortable or awkward. "So, when are Jasper and Sheila going to finally get together?"

"What do you mean?"

"I mean, I hope it's okay to talk about this. They're both our friends, and it's obvious they like each other."

"Oh, it's okay, but they *are* together."

I tilted my head and leaned back. "They are? Did I miss something?"

"You didn't hear about it? Jasper showed up at Sheila's dance class two weeks ago, cleaned up, hair trimmed, gelled and neat—in a very nice suit, with long-stem roses—and asked her to dance. He looked like a new man—Jasper cleans up well. And I'll tell you one more thing—that *new man* sure can dance. I can't believe you didn't know this. He literally swept her off her feet!"

"You're kidding me. That old dog!"

Why didn't he tell me about this?

Chapter 20

C oach Jasper did something before the all-star game that he hadn't done all season, including the playoffs. He showed up early. The kids who knew him joked about it, and they also pointed out how neatly his hair was combed.

"Coach, what's up with you lately? You're like a different guy," Nolan asked.

"He's got a girlfriend now—my mom!" shouted Pip.

Most of the other kids on the all-star team were from different teams than Pip and Nolan, and they didn't get why any of that was funny. But our three kids roared with laughter. We'd all been speculating, all season, on when Coach Jasper and Sheila would finally admit they liked each other.

"Nolan, come over here with me and Coach Barrett. I wanna discuss somethin' with you 'bout next season," Jasper requested.

Nolan and I followed Jasper a few yards away from the bench for a little privacy. I had no idea what the discussion would be about.

"Son, I talked to the Lackton Youth Baseball board, and the head of Kipford Little League—and your father was involved, too."

Nolan's smile dropped, and he rolled his eyes. He looked at me, and put his palms up.

I just shrugged. I had no idea what Jasper was about to say.

Coach Jasper continued, "Kipford's gonna open up their preseason draft to a few kids from Lackton next year. You'll definitely be one of 'em."

"I don't wanna play with those jerks," Nolan protested. "All they care about is winning, and nothing else—just like my dad. What about all that stuff you're always saying, about winning not being everything, and picking up your teammates? Now you're gonna send me to Kipford? That doesn't make any sense, coach."

"They're not jerks, they're just kids, like you, and everyone else playin' ball today. They are definitely more competitive over there, but you're a special ball player, son. I think the extra competition would be good for you."

"Why are you doing this? I don't wanna play for a Kipford team. I wanna stay on your team next year."

"Well, to be perfectly honest, there ain't nothin' more I can teach you on a baseball field that'd help you get better. You don't have to change, or go back to being all about winnin', but you should be working hard and challengin' yourself. They got better coachin', better facilities…I mean, just look at our field. This place is barely suitable for a dog park."

"I think it's a great opportunity for you, Nolan. You can work hard on your game, and still keep it fun. That's always going to be up to you, regardless of who you play with," I added.

"You don't have to make a decision now, but think about it. I believe you have a future in baseball. This is the best option for you," Jasper insisted.

Nolan looked over at his teammates, and then scanned the field. He looked like he was already considering the move.

"You know, Kipford has sent more than one team to the Little League World Series over the years? You won't get there playin' in Lackton, I promise you that," Coach Jasper admitted.

Nolan nodded. He was beginning to see Jasper's point.

"Now get out there and warm up. Let's show those Kipford boys what we got, and why they're gonna want you next year."

Nolan ran out onto the field to join his team, and Jasper stopped me before I trotted out to follow him.

"So, you finally took Miss Lauren out on a date. It's about time, buddy. How'd that go?"

"Better than I'd ever imagined it would," I started, but then I toned it down a notch, and played it cool. "It was nice—it was real nice."

Jasper smiled, and let out a chuckle.

"And why didn't you tell me you'd gone through with our plan to impress Sheila at her dance class? You pulled off the *grand gesture,* man! I heard you swept her right off her feet—literally."

"That's 'cause of two reasons. One, I didn't wanna put any pressure on you to take out Miss Lauren. And, two, I'm a gentleman—and gentlemen never tell."

I laughed. "Well, I'm happy for you—for both of you."

"Likewise, my friend," Jasper replied.

"Hey! Look who came to watch our kids play," I said, and pointed out Miss Tammy and her new man, Mason.

Miss Tammy waved and winked.

"I think she's still got a thing for you, Jasper," I speculated.

"Shoot, she looks great, buddy. If I wasn't spoken for, I'd—naw, man, no I wouldn't"

"Yeah, you would," I joked.

"Forget that. How 'bout we get these kids ready to pull off a little miracle?"

The all-star games between Lackton Youth Baseball and the Kipford Little League minors and majors had been played for eighteen straight seasons. Kipford had won all eighteen years at both levels—and the games were hardly ever close. But the Lackton teams showed up to play, every year, to take their pounding, every year. It would definitely take a small miracle to change that. Could Nolan Pickett be the miracle we needed?

Nolan pitched like a young man with something to prove, and managed to get us all the way to the last inning with a two-run lead.

The elation felt by the Lackton crowd was short-lived, however, because when we turned to backup pitching for the top half of the final inning, we gave up three runs, and we entered the bottom half of the inning down by one. Nolan had stayed in the game and played left field. We needed his bat.

Down by just one run, our team rallied, and the bases were loaded with only one out. Nolan Pickett stood on third base and watched our second best hitter strike out at the plate for the second out.

You could hear a collective moan from the home crowd. And their hopes seemed fully dashed when Pip, who had just entered the game to play right field in the prior half inning, came to the plate, dragging an over-sized bat behind him.

"Pinch hitter!" shouted one of the fathers in the crowd.

"Come on, coach. We can win this thing!" yelled another.

Before a pitch was thrown, Nolan had sprung into action from third base. He started shouting to get the pitcher's attention, and took a massive lead toward home.

The pitcher stepped toward him and lifted the baseball to show he was ready to try and throw Nolan out.

"Don't you throw that ball, Blake! Just look him back to third. He wants you to throw it!" the Kipford coach yelled from the visiting team's bench.

The pitcher faked a throw, but Nolan didn't move a muscle, maintaining his giant lead toward home plate. And then he took another step toward home.

"Don't do it!" the Kipford coach repeated. "Strike this batter out, and let's go home."

The rattled pitcher turned his back to Nolan and stepped back to the top of the pitching mound.

The moment the pitcher's eyes were off of him, Nolan bolted toward home.

Even if the throw was on target, and it wasn't close, Nolan would have been safe by a mile. And our baserunners on first and second advanced to second and third on the awkward throw to home plate that rolled to the backstop.

Nolan had tied the game, and the game-winning run had advanced to third base.

Pip, who had stepped away from the plate to make room for Nolan's sliding steal, came over to give his friend a high five. "You did it! We're tied now."

"Now you listen to me, Pip. There's no pressure on you right now. The game is tied, and even if we finish with a tie, this town will go nuts. Lackton hasn't ever given Kipford a game like this."

Pip furrowed his brow, and looked toward the bench. "Won't we go into extra innings?" he asked.

"This is an exhibition game. There's no extra innings in an exhibition," Nolan insisted. "Now forget all that nonsense my father told you about not swinging, and hoping for a walk. Swing that bat! I know you can do it."

"Young man, please return to your bench and let's play ball," the umpire said.

"You got this, Pip. Get a hit, buddy," Nolan added, and started walking off the field, as instructed.

"Time out!" yelled the Kipford coach, and he went out to the mound to talk with his pitcher.

When Nolan was back with the team, on the bench, Jasper looked at me and started to suggest, "You know, they ain't thrown a pitch yet, we still could put in a pinch…"

"Don't you even dream of it!" Nolan interrupted.

Jasper just winked at me, and then nodded in agreement with Nolan.

"Maybe I did teach you a little somethin' this year," Coach Jasper said quietly to Nolan. Then he cupped his hands over his mouth and yelled toward home plate, "Let's go! Swing that bat, Pip!"

Nolan sat beside me, on the bench. "No matter what happens next, this will always be my favorite season playing baseball."

"Tell me that when you're playing for the Cubs," I replied.

"Cubs? To heck with the Cubs! I'll be playing against the Cubs!"

"Why does everyone around here hate my Cubs?"

"Um, maybe it's because we're all Cardinals fans," Nolan answered.

"Let's be ready to take the field if Pip strikes out, boys. We can take this in extra innings." Jasper told the team.

"There ain't gonna be no extra innings, coach," Nolan insisted. "Pip's gonna get a hit. Plus, I told him this was an exhibition, and exhibitions don't go into extra innings—so he'd feel a little less pressure."

Coach Jasper chuckled. "You think Kipford would ever walk away with a tie score? We'd be here all night 'fore that happened."

"Play ball!" shouted the umpire.

Pip smiled and waved to his mother and Aunt Lauren in the crowd, and then stepped into the batter's box with a bat that was much too big for him resting on his shoulder.

"Oh Lord, please don't let him get hit by another pitch," Sheila prayed.

"Eyes on the ball and swing!" Coach Jasper shouted.

Pip made contact with the very first pitch he faced, and the ball dropped straight to the ground, in front of home plate.

Everyone froze, including the Kipford fielders.

"RUN!" Nolan shouted from the bench.

Pip dropped his bat and took off for first base.

"Get the ball to first! Now!" yelled the Kipford coach.

The catcher scrambled to take off his mask and find the ball.

"Throw it!" yelled the Kipford coach. "Throw it to first base! Right now!"

The frazzled young catcher tossed the ball over the first baseman's head while Pip was still a few steps away from first base.

Pip had his first and only hit, ever, and the baserunner on third easily made it home before the first baseman could recover the ball and attempt to throw him out at home plate.

Pip ran over first base, and then turned and hopped back onto it to claim his prize.

Coaches, players, and parents rushed Lackton Field and surrounded poor Pip, who wasn't quite ready for so much attention.

Nolan rescued his friend and hoisted him up on his shoulders to take a victory lap around the bases.

There were cheers, and plenty of tears, while all of the Lackton all-star players, and some of their parents, followed close behind the duo of Nolan and Pip around the bases, shouting, "Center Bench! Center Bench! Center Bench!"

Chapter 21
Present Day

More than a decade has passed since that magical day on Lackton Field. And though Kipford Little League had kept its promise to include Lackton's top talent in their preseason draft, the annual all-star game between Kipford Little League and Lackton Youth Baseball continued—and with the added talent, Kipford started a new and even more one-sided reign of dominance over Lackton.

Pip went to that writing camp in Texas that he had won admission to, and we wrote letters to each other every day like we'd discussed. I could see the progress in his writing skills with every letter that he sent me.

My young friend didn't play another season of baseball, electing to spend summers focusing on his writing instead. He was invited back to that same writing camp every year, tuition free, until he graduated high school.

From there, he went to the University of Texas to earn a Liberal Arts degree and his Master of Fine Arts in Creative Writing.

Pip worked on his *Space Lordz* series through high school and college and it was published before he graduated from UT. The series eventually became a huge hit. He's an internationally acclaimed best-selling author now, and there's talk of *Space Lordz* becoming a cartoon series on a cable TV network.

Even though Pip quit baseball, he and Nolan Pickett remain close friends to this day.

After our wildly unexpected win at Lackton Field, Nolan played the next two seasons with Kipford Little League. In year two, Nolan and the rest of the Kipford all-stars made a run at the Little League World Series in Williamsport, Pennsylvania.

Nolan led his team to the final eight, but they were stopped there. Though he didn't make it to the championship, Nolan's talent earned him plenty of attention, and a few years later he was drafted by the St. Louis Cardinals right out of high school. He worked his way through the minors and eventually to a spot in the Cardinal's bullpen as a relief pitcher.

Once Pip had decided to quit playing baseball, Jasper retired from coaching. He and Sheila were married shortly after, which was our second wedding that season—Miss Tammy and Mason had tied the knot a few weeks before.

We've all moved out of Rolling Meadows—Jasper was the most reluctant to make the change. Last year, Pip bought his mother and Jasper a house in Kipford as a late wedding present, and though Jasper was grateful for the very generous gift he wasn't thrilled about the idea of becoming a Kipford resident.

He's doing just fine now—he finally got his old Camaro "purrin' like a kitten," and he enjoys showing it off to his fancy new friends in Kipford.

I suppose that leaves just Lauren and me. We've been happily living together in Kipford for the last eight years, and I'm about to pop the question—and not just because Jasper has been bugging me forever to do so.

Jasper isn't wrong though, and even I can't believe I've waited so many years to finally propose to such an amazing woman, who I love with all my heart. Lauren helped me to get back to the man I was before losing Charlotte and David.

My love for Lauren, and some much needed therapy, motivated me to put all of the broken pieces of my heart and life back together. I haven't stopped missing Charlotte and David—and no one expects me to—but I've found the strength to move forward and find the happiness I need, and deserve, for the rest of my life. I carry them with me everywhere I go.

Shortly after the all-star game, I quit my job at the sawmill and started a new career in investments at a firm in Kipford. It feels good to do something I'm more comfortable with and much better suited to do.

I've also become pretty active in the community. I'm doing volunteer work, and I even tried my hand in local politics. I almost won my first election, but just a few days before the vote my opponent very wisely informed the voters that I was actually from Chicago. After that, my campaign, along with any other political ambitions I'd considered in Oklahoma, were finished forever.

I'm happy to report that I've reconnected with Charlotte's parents, at Lauren's insistence. We've visited them, in Chicago, several times over the years, and we're actually in Chicago now. We're about to pick them up to bring them to a very special event—more about that in a moment.

Charlotte's parents are aware, and overjoyed, that I'm planning to ask Lauren to marry me tonight during our big evening. In some small way, their blessing serves as the final okay from Charlotte for me to move on, and I'm thrilled to have it.

There is something I haven't mentioned—I'm writing a book. After Pip had become a famous author, I told him he should write a book about our amazing summer and the miracle all-star victory. He said that would be a great story, but it wasn't his genre—he suggested I should give it a try. So, I'm working on it, slowly. I'm just applying the finishing touches and then we'll see how it goes.

Back to our big plans for tonight. Pip managed to get a luxury box for the whole gang—Lauren and me, Sheila and Jasper, Miss Tammy and Mason, and of course Charlotte's parents—at tonight's game six of the World Series between the Chicago White Sox and the St. Louis Cardinals. We're all very excited to see Pip there, too—it's been too long.

As I've mentioned, baseball isn't the only thing on tonight's agenda for me. I've got the ring in my pocket, and I'll get down on one knee during the seventh inning stretch—wish me luck.

Jasper had asked me if I was bummed out about seeing the White Sox tonight, and not my beloved Cubs, in the World Series. My answer: "To heck with the Cubs, and their poser fans. And to heck with the

White Sox, too. I'm rooting for my friend, Nolan Pickett, and my new home team. Check out my fancy new hat, buddy. I'm rooting for the Cardinals!"

Acknowledgments

My love for writing has grown to more of an obsession, and at times, or maybe all of the time, I talk about make-believe people doing make-believe things with the people I cherish the most who are busy living their actual lives in the actual world. As always, I want to give a heartfelt thank you, and I love you, to my wife, Renee, and children, Emily and Austin, for consistently putting up with my obsession and encouraging me for these past several years.

Thank you to my parents and to my much older, and less visually appealing siblings, for recognizing that I was a little different, and for not trying too hard to beat the normal back into me. All kidding aside, nothing makes me happier than the support my brothers and sisters have shown me since I began this crazy journey. I wouldn't want to do any of it without you. I love you guys.

A special thank you to Steve Pascucci for listening to my brief and illogical description of what I believed the imaginary Lackton Field looks like, and then knocking it out of the park—pun intended! Thank you for the fantastic cover art. I couldn't be happier with it. Steve is a very talented artist and can be hired for private lessons, or paint parties, by looking up Art Made Easely on Facebook. He comes very well recommended. I hope this is the first of many projects we work on together.

And because there can never be too much beautiful art in the world, or in one of my books, I wanted to give my sincere thanks to Cathy Schilling. Cathy is responsible for the wonderful art opposite the first page of Chapter 1, which is another perspective of Lackton Field. Cathy and I live in the same town, and I hope we'll run into one another from time to time. Thank you for helping to make this book more beautiful.

A final thank you to Dennis Kouba. Though I've gotten much, much better over the last few years, I'm far from perfect. Thank you for keeping me honest, helping to make me look better, and for making sure all my commas are in the right place. I've never admitted this before, but you are the reason I'm now a firm believer in the Oxford comma. Thank you for that!

Also by Brian D. Campbell

The Third King: Coronation
Part I of the Ben Gilsum Book Series
(Red Cliff Press, 2018)

Guardian Angel: True Calling
Part II of the Ben Gilsum Book Series
(Red Cliff Press, 2019)

Denying The Stylus
A Novella by Brian D. Campbell
(Red Cliff Press, 2020)

For More Information

Visit our website:
www.redcliffpress.wordpress.com